LOVE, MUSIC, MADNESS

TABITHA RHYS

SOUL MATE PUBLISHING

New York

LOVE, MUSIC, MADNESS

Copyright©2018

TABITHA RHYS

Cover Design by Leah Kaye-Suttle

Published in the United States of America by
Soul Mate Publishing
P.O. Box 24
Macedon, New York, 14502

ISBN: 978-1-68291-697-1

ebook ISBN: 978-1-68291-655-1

www.SoulMatePublishing.com

To all the artists,

musicians,

and wanderers I've met,

however briefly.

Acknowledgments

Thank you to Lori Polito and Deborah Gilbert at Soul Mate Publishing, and to my patient and insightful beta readers, especially Phillip, Brittany, Josh, and Idore. Further thanks to cover artist Leah Kaye Suttle.

Chapter 1

I had no idea why Jessa Warlow wanted to meet with me. For one thing, I hardly knew her. She was one of my brother's friends back in high school, but I hadn't seen her for years. Besides that, Jessa is what I can only call Gunther, Pennsylvania royalty. It's not just that she's pretty in an old movie star kind of way. She's also an artist, and a singer. Everybody in town always swore she'd be on the radio someday. I couldn't imagine she'd have time to meet up with an old friend's kid brother for nostalgic purposes only.

I found Jessa's choice of location just as perplexing. The windows of the bar were blacked out—porno-shop style— and the only patrons under fifty were some greasy rockabilly kids slinking around by the pool tables. In the back of the room, a massive jukebox threw off a radioactive glow, but even that saving grace had been ruined. The rockabilly bastards were playing Morrissey on loop.

I figured Jessa would clear up all my questions as soon as she arrived. The problem was, I'd been parked on a barstool for nearly twenty minutes and she still hadn't shown. Chances were, she'd changed her mind. Of course, if she had, I wouldn't know it. I'd never been able to convince myself to shell out for a cell phone, so any last-minute cancellation messages would only end up on the answering machine back at my mother's house.

After another five minutes alone in a bar redolent of fresh vomit and ancient cigarettes, all I could do was pull my trusty corduroy jacket over my hoodie and prepare to make my exit. But I was too hasty. The second I touched one foot down onto the stained carpet, a hand locked on my wrist.

I looked up in surprise—and straight into Jessa Warlow's unmistakable cat-like eyes.

She narrowed them and smiled. "Lawson Harper?"

"At, uh . . . at your service," I said with only a slight stutter.

"I knew it!" Jessa released me and slid onto the barstool to my right. "Though I must say, you look quite different from the last time I saw you. You know, back when you and your little sister used to sit in the kitchen eating peanut butter sandwiches—while your brother's friends filled your tiny lungs with second-hand smoke."

I laughed, careful to keep my mouth closed so as not to reveal a set of teeth nobody would want to show off, and gave Jessa a once-over. She had changed too. Her sandy hair, which once fell in a tangle down her back, was now cut neatly at her shoulders. She was also dressed more smartly than I remembered—in a sweater dress and a military-style coat—but her face was still the same. Heart-shaped, with those feline eyes.

"Going to tell me what we're doing here?" I asked as I cast my gaze around the bar.

She shrugged. "What can I say? I don't want to run into any of my old friends tonight."

I couldn't imagine why Jessa Warlow would want to hide out. If her friends knew she was in town, I was pretty sure they would roll out the red carpet.

"Of course," Jessa went on, "you're probably wondering why I wanted to meet with you at all."

I was. But I had to wait for my answer because, very suddenly, a bug-eyed bloke of a bartender planted his arms in front of us and raised his brows expectantly.

"Gin and tonic," Jessa tossed out.

I asked for a rum and cola as smoothly as I could. I'd only been twenty-one for a few months, and I didn't want to come off like a kid. Or an amateur.

If I did, Jessa—who would have been twenty-five, same as my brother—didn't appear to notice. As soon as the barkeep moved off, she turned back my way. "The first thing I should tell you is that I'm not here in Gunther for a visit. I quit my job in Philadelphia and moved back home just last week."

That was a surprise. If I ever found a way to get out of Gunther, I'd never come back. Not in a million years. "Why?"

"I had a good job in the design department of a big company, but it wasn't creative—and I want to be creative again. Very badly. I also want to take another shot at a career as a musician. A serious one this time."

When the bartender set down our cocktails, cold and sweating, I reached for my wallet.

Jessa knocked my hand away. "I invited you here. I pay."

I let her. Mostly because I wanted to hear more. Especially the part that had to do with me. "What do you mean by 'serious'?" I pressed.

"In high school and college, I was always in a rush, too eager to get out in front of a crowd. This time, I want to build out and polish my songs. I want to record them. Make a real record." Jessa stirred her drink fiercely. "You still play the guitar?"

I watched her ice cubes chase each other around the glass. "I do." Work and school kept me running, but most nights I fell asleep playing along to one of the old cassettes my father left behind when he skipped town. Sometimes it was the only way I could get my mind quiet.

"Then perhaps," she said, "you'd like to help me out."

It took me a few beats to fully comprehend that Jessa

Warlow was asking me to write music with her, when I never expected she would remember I played music at all.

I suppressed a smile. "I want to help," I told her. "The only problem is, I'm not much of a songwriter."

Jessa considered. "Well, I've got lyrics, melodies, chords. All I really need is a guitarist who can add some interesting leads. Maybe a breakdown or two." She pointed her plastic stirrer in my direction. "We could always meet up for a session at my place and see how it goes. I mean, if you're interested."

"I'm interested," I said, careful not to sound *too* interested. You know, not creepy-interested. Or desperate-interested. "When did you want to get together?"

I felt Jessa's eyes brush over me. "How about now?"

"Now? As in right this minute?"

"Unless you want to stay and finish that drink." She peered into my tepid rum and cola. "How is it anyway?"

"I haven't had any."

"Oh good." Jessa's hand locked down on my wrist for the second time that night. "Then you can drive."

Chapter 2

The heater in the little Nissan I shared with my sister Allison was on the fritz, but Jessa bore the cold bravely as I navigated the streets of town. We cruised past Ralphie's (where I spent most of my nights assembling pizzas for the good people of Gunther), the post office, and the several vaguely Irish bars that lined Main Street. At the corner, I turned onto my street—a residential artery lined on both sides with the kind of modest homes Allison used to call "shoebox houses."

The Warlows lived behind my family's place in a subdivision full of sturdy brick homes and lined with elms so old their branches twisted together in the middle of the street. I wasn't sure which place was hers, but Jessa kindly pointed it out and I brought the car to a stop at the curb. When I saw her house rising up against the inky sky, a little thrill passed through me.

It felt strange, and more than a little bit exciting, to be going inside the Warlow home for the first time. I figured I'd spend the latter part of my evening alone in my basement bedroom, counting the pipes on the ceiling. Instead, I was going to make music with Jessa Warlow, the girl everybody wanted to hear on the radio.

"Your parents won't mind that we're getting started so late?" I asked as we hoofed it up the driveway. My breath came out in white puffs that rose into the night sky like little ghosts.

Jessa shook her head. "I've always worked on music at

all hours. They're either heavy sleepers, or very supportive." She shot me a wry half-smile. "Probably both."

After Jessa unlocked the front door, I followed her into the dim foyer and up a set of creaky wooden steps. While I stood in the doorway to her bedroom, breathing in the comforting scents of old carpet and clove cigarettes, she studied a collection of guitars on stands in the corner.

"Here." Jessa passed a shiny Taylor my way and chose a scuffed Crafter for herself.

I watched her sink down to the mustard shag, then did the same.

"Play anything," I said as I grabbed a pick from a little brass bowl on the floor. "I'll jump in."

Jessa nodded and began to strum. Her progression was simple—four chords, with a changeup at the end of the phrase—but her chord choices were unexpected. They were jazzy-sounding. Joni Mitchell style. I watched the unusual shapes Jessa's fingers made on the strings, then joined in.

A few measures later, Jessa began to hum, then sing. Her singing voice was not unlike her speaking voice, but it was much warmer and fuller. Sort of gravelly and velvety at the same time.

I listened intently. When I got a feel for the song, I complemented Jessa's vocal melody with a little finger-picking. Then I added a turnaround.

She stopped. "You're good."

I reddened. "Solid maybe."

"No," she said. "Really incredible. I could never pick up a new song so quickly. Where did you learn?"

"My dad taught me." That was before he started hating my guts. Neither Thom nor Allison had been patient enough to sit still and follow his gruff instructions. But I always kept up, and kept quiet.

"Let's go again," Jessa urged. "I'd like to work out this song a little more. Then maybe we'll try another."

I nodded and raised my pick. I couldn't think of anything I'd rather do.

~ ~ ~

Over the course of several hours, Jessa and I pulled apart three of her songs and put them back together. The first two were soft and jazzy. The last was bluesy and thundering. When Jessa forgot a lyric, she referred to an old composition book she produced from under her bed. I couldn't read most of the words that were scrawled over every inch, but she had no trouble deciphering the scribbles.

It was nearly two a.m. when we finally called it quits. By then, Jessa and I had three respectable rough drafts recorded on her phone. "That went rather well," Jessa said.

"It did."

"Perhaps it's something we'll do again."

"I hope so." That was an understatement. I hadn't felt so creative—or so accomplished—in a long time. I'd never thought of myself as a songwriter, but taking what Jessa had already made and layering on top of it came easy to me. I couldn't wait to do it again.

I sensed Jessa's eyes following me as I got to my feet and placed her Taylor carefully on its stand. "Hey," she said, hugging her knees to her chest, "would you mind not telling anybody that we met up tonight?"

"No problem." I shrugged. "Any special reason?"

She hesitated. "I'm sort of laying low."

"What do you mean?"

"I haven't told any of my friends I'm back in town." She sighed. "You see, I don't want anybody to know that I quit my job. Or that I'm living here with my parents. Not until I have a record—or at least more to show for this move back home. Does that make sense?"

"Perfect sense." It did. Although I hadn't suspected

Jessa Warlow would care what her friends thought of her. Or anybody for that matter.

I moved to retrieve my jacket from her bed, where I'd tossed it mid-session. Then something occurred to me. If Jessa was intent on hiding out, she would probably want to know that my brother was coming to town. Mostly because that meant those hiding out days were numbered.

If Jessa had once been Gunther's queen, my brother Thom had just as surely been king—a role he savored and was likely to resume upon arrival. As soon as Thom got to Gunther, old friends, and friends of friends, would start coming around again. No doubt about it.

I wasn't sure I wanted to give Jessa what might be received as bad news. At the same time, I knew she would find out eventually and wonder why I hadn't given her a heads up.

"If you haven't talked to your friends, then I guess nobody told you my brother's visiting after Christmas," I said slowly.

Just as I hoped it wouldn't, Jessa's smile faded. "Thom is coming here? To Gunther? You can't be serious."

All she had to do was look at me to know I was.

"Hasn't Thom been out in California for the last four years?"

"He has."

Jessa bristled. "So, why now?"

"He claims to miss Gunther. He claims to miss my mom, and my sister, and me."

Jessa raised herself from the floor and put her guitar back on its stand with jerky motions. "I see. I guess I won't be 'laying low' much longer."

"Sorry," I said, "I shouldn't have brought it up."

"I'm glad you did," Jessa insisted. But she didn't sound glad. Not at all.

By then, I was wishing very hard that I had kept quiet.

Jessa and I had just completed a near-perfect session—we were on the brink of scheduling a follow-up rehearsal, I was sure of it—and I had gone and made myself the bearer of bad news.

I tried to think of something encouraging to say, but couldn't come up with anything that wouldn't sound fake or forced. I reached for my jacket and got ready to say a speedy goodnight.

But before I could get anything out, something unexpected happened.

Jessa stepped toward me, eyes narrowed. Then she grabbed a handful of my T-shirt. And crushed her lips against my lips.

I couldn't have been more surprised. All I could think was that she had made some kind of mistake. I expected her to jump back, muttering excuses, any second.

She didn't.

Instead, she yanked me closer.

Without meaning to, I dropped my jacket and let out a little gasp. That was all it took to be making out, with tongue and everything.

The warm delirium hit me all at once, like a wave, and I hardly knew what I was doing. There was an acute loneliness inside of me at that time in my life and, as it turned out, Jessa's embrace was like a salve. I pressed against her with a desperation I didn't know I had, and she pressed back against me just as fiercely.

When she gave me a little shove, I let myself fall back onto her little twin bed. Jessa came with me, and our bodies connected in a way that sent a jolt of electricity through my insides. I guess she felt it too because she began throwing my hoodie off my shoulders in an incredible hurry.

"This thing is pretty threadbare," she said breathlessly. "I'm shocked it doesn't come apart in the wash." Then she was tugging at my belt.

I knew what that meant, of course, and I knew it was no time to hesitate or act shy. I didn't want Jessa to get the idea I was some inexperienced kid brother type and call the whole thing off. So, doing my best to seem capable and mature, I produced a condom from my wallet. And then, with just a few turns and noisy re-adjustments, there we were, screwing on Jessa's lumpy twin with most of our clothes on.

Jessa was intensely beautiful with her sandy hair all spilled out on the pillow and her eyelashes fanning down in a neat row.

I couldn't make myself look away.

Then the bed springs squealed. I tried to shift, but Jessa's boots kept getting tangled up in my jeans.

Moments later, we turned over and Jessa was on top of me with her hands on my chest. That's when I grabbed the pillow out from under my head and mashed it as hard as I could against my face. Just like that, the whole thing was over.

I guess you could say I was stunned. It wasn't as if I'd never taken a girl to bed, but this was Jessa Warlow. She was practically famous—at least in Gunther—and we'd just had a songwriting session, not a date. I didn't know what to do, or what to say to her. So I just laid there like an idiot, or a corpse, while she straightened out her clothes.

Fortunately, Jessa seemed to have an idea about what would happen next. "Think you could drive me back to the bar?" she asked, as if nothing had happened that might warrant comment or concern. She stretched her back like a cat. "I left my parents' car in the lot."

I sat up quickly and tried to appear composed. "Uh, yes. Of course I will."

Jessa stood and eyed me expectantly, but I didn't move. "It would probably be best if I had it back before they wake up."

"Right." I scrambled to my feet.

Chapter 3

I honestly didn't think I'd hear from Jessa ever again. Our late-night encounter was simply too strange and too sudden—too obviously driven by a fit of impulse. I pictured running into Jessa in the grocery store and making brief eye contact over some broccoli, or pulling up next to her at a red light and sharing a knowing smile. That, I figured, would be the extent of our interactions.

Or at least that's what I told myself. I didn't want to get my hopes up. Hopes can be dangerous things. One minute they're bobbing on the horizon like hundreds of brightly-colored zeppelins. The next, the sky is full of Hindenburgs, burning down to their metal skeletons and falling to the earth in flames.

When my best friend and loyal companion Matthew Brewer asked me where I'd been all weekend, I took care not to mention Jessa Warlow or the dive bar where we'd rendezvoused. "I was working," I told him as I slid into one of the Gunther Bowl's sticky yellow chairs. That wasn't a lie. I had closed on Friday, opened on Saturday, and taken a shift on Sunday afternoon when one of the cooks called out.

Matt didn't press me further. I knew he didn't ask me to meet at the local bowling alley, our old haunt, to find out what I'd been up to—or just to indulge in the Gunther Bowl's famously cheap beers. The fact was, there was a question I had been dodging for quite some time. And I owed Matt an answer.

The lamps overhead burned with an uncomfortable

brightness, and I found myself longing for the dark of a bar. Blacked-out windows optional.

But Matt didn't start in on his questioning right away. He arched an eyebrow and gestured to the bowling team in the lanes ahead of us.

I wasn't generally keen on watching middle-aged men sweat through their polyester, but Matt had long been intrigued by the copious perspiration the local bowling team produced in factory proportions. For him, the massive patches of sweat that brightened every league shirt held particular fascination. He took pleasure in interpreting their shapes, the way you might an inkblot test or clouds in the sky.

The corners of Matt's mouth curled upward as he eyed the moistened back of the gentleman who had just stepped up to the line. "Is it just me, or is that a perfect bust of Benjamin Franklin?" The bowler raised his arm. "And that's Eli Whitney. With his cotton gin."

I shook my head. "No way. That's Sergeant Pepper's Lonely Hearts Club Band. In full uniformed regalia."

"Good one." Matt reached out his fist to touch mine. Then he sat back and took a deep breath. The fun and games were over. "Hey," he said, "you aren't going to transfer with me in the fall, are you?"

I stared at the floor. "No," I confirmed. "I'm not."

I braced myself for Matt's reaction, but he remained silent. The continuous thunder-roll of bowling balls careening down the lanes was suddenly deafening in my ears. "Did you hear . . ."

"I figured," he interrupted. "I mean, you've been putting me off for a while now, Lawson. It's not like I didn't notice."

I knew I owed Matt an explanation, especially since we'd been planning our university days since junior high. Matt was only slumming it at Gunther Community College because he was waiting on me. "It's not that I don't want to. But my mom hasn't finished her book, and I don't think she's going to any time soon. Her writing hasn't brought in any money in more than a year."

Matt rocked slowly in his chair. He was trying to play cool and collected, but I could practically hear his molars grinding. "Your mom's an adult, and writing's her job. If she doesn't want to do her job, isn't that on her?"

"Allison won't graduate for three more years," I reminded Matt. I wasn't taking care of the bills for my mom's sake. I wanted my sister to have a stable home so she could get decent grades and then go to a decent school with the rest of her friends. Not that I expected Matt to understand. His parents had their shit together.

Matt kicked at the leg of his chair. He seemed to be searching for a last-ditch appeal. "Most people who take time off never go back, Lawson."

I finally looked my best friend straight in the eye. I could locate no trace of humor in his baby browns. It was weird seeing Matt so serious. Mainly due to the fact that he was almost never serious. "Sorry," I said. "I just can't swing it."

The words seemed to land between us with a final thud. Then other words—like "dropout" and "loser"—started circling in my head.

I guess they were circling in Matt's head too, because he was suddenly excusing himself. "You know, I should get going. My parents are expecting me for dinner."

Considering Matt's parents both worked late and left him money for takeout almost every night, that was very unlikely. "No worries," I told him anyway. "We'll get together some other time." That, I knew, was also unlikely.

Matt had clearly written me off as one of those guys you can't help till he helps himself. And there wasn't a damn thing I could do about it.

~ ~ ~

When I got home from work that night, all I wanted to do was drop onto my mattress and sleep off what had been a very long day. After letting down my best friend since grade three, I'd gone straight to Ralphie's Pizzeria, where I had to work on the line with two brand new guys who didn't know ass from elbow. Just as I was heaving myself into bed in all my clothes, the phone upstairs rang loud and shrill. I pulled my pillow over my head, hoping Allison would answer it, but answer she did not. I waited out the ringing, but after a sweet five seconds of silence, the ringing started right up again.

Resigned, I trudged upstairs and grabbed the phone from its place next to the stove. "Hello?" I intoned, perhaps a little too fiercely. I couldn't begin to imagine who would be calling the house line at such an hour.

The caller paused. "Uh . . . am I disturbing you?"

The receiver went ice cold in my hand. The voice on the line didn't belong to one of Allison's overzealous suitors or some mouth-breathing crank caller. It was Jessa's.

"Am I calling too late?" she asked. "Back in high school, your mother never cared when any of us called the house."

I forced myself to form words. "It's not too late." My mother had never kept regular hours. Even before she began shutting herself up in her room for most of the day.

"Glad to hear it. Can you rehearse tonight?"

"Sure." I struggled to keep my voice steady. "What time?"

"When can you get here?"

"Fifteen minutes," I told her. Although I was pretty sure I could get there in ten.

After a quick goodbye, I balled up my apron, hurried down into the basement to change my shirt, and then I was out the door. I didn't even have to go back upstairs. When my dad lived at our house, he had installed a basement door that led straight outside so he could come and go without the inconvenience of associating with his wife and children.

By the time I stepped into the back yard, I had already decided to make the trek to Jessa's place on foot. The distance was shorter that way—the narrow strip of woods behind my house led directly to her subdivision—and if she wanted to lay low, having my car in her driveway wouldn't help her cause.

All the way to Jessa's house, the bitter cold seeped through my jacket and my hoodie, and into my bones, but I hardly noticed. While I dodged branches and picked thorns out of my jeans, I told myself all I wanted to do was make music with Jessa Warlow. I wanted to try my hand at songwriting. I wanted to be creative. I didn't care if Jessa was into me. And I certainly didn't care whether she would want to do terrible and wonderful things with me on her scratchy purple afghan ever again.

Those were all, of course, bald-faced lies. But they kept me calm, and they kept me sane.

~ ~ ~

That night, Jessa and I revisited the songs we worked on during our last session. We solidified the new parts for her bluesy barnburner and built out her ballad with a bridge. The third song we took in a completely different direction by replacing Jessa's strummed verses with a sparse lead I came up with on the spot.

The whole time I forced myself not to wonder whether what happened after our last session would happen again. I told myself there was no chance. That Jessa had just given in to an impulse—a whim. That it didn't mean anything. But after our session had concluded and I set my guitar down, I felt Jessa's arms slipping under mine. Then her lips were scraping across my collarbone.

I squeezed my eyes shut as a scorching heat surged through me, all the way to my fingertips. For a few seconds, I let myself absorb what was happening. I could hardly make myself believe it. Then I knew. I was going to be Jessa Warlow's guitarist. I was also going to be the warm body standing between her and loneliness at a peculiar, in-between time in her life. It would probably be temporary, and it would probably mean much more to me than it did to her.

That was all right. It was *more* than all right. I would take what I would get. Because Jessa was beautiful, and unapologetic, and an artist. To me, she was irresistible. With Jessa in my arms and in my life, I didn't care about my forsaken college plans, and I didn't care about my hellish work schedule. And I (almost) didn't care that Christmas was coming.

~ ~ ~

I am aware that in most homes the Christmas season is a time for joy. In mine, however, it is a nightmare. Set to the soundtrack of Fleetwood Mac. A few days before the big holiday, my mom starts looping all the records she bought back when she and my dad first got together. A few days after that, something much worse happens—my father shows up.

We don't hear much from him for the rest of the year, but my dad insists on braving the I-95 gridlock every Christmas Eve so we can all play family for a day. I guess it's so he can pretend he's a good father to Allison. And so he doesn't haven't to admit that he failed. And maybe so my mother won't move on, which would be too much for his fragile ego.

That year, my dad made his big entrance just before midnight. I was lying on my bed, playing guitar along with an old cassette when I sensed somebody else in the room. I opened up my eyes and there was his ruddy moonface.

I removed my headphones. I knew what was coming. I'd moved out of my brother Thom's old room and into the basement after school started, and I knew my father wouldn't like it. In the last two years before he left for good, the basement had been his domain.

"You've really settled in, haven't you?" my dad asked. His eyes darted around the room, taking in the shoeboxes full of old tapes and CDs next to my bed, and the school books piled on the dresser.

"I get more studying done down here." My grades were the one thing he'd never been able to criticize. I always made A's and B's.

My dad glanced right, then left, clearly casting around for something else to complain about. "Well, get the tree ready, will you?" he said finally. "I know you couldn't give two shits about Christmas, but you're old enough to start thinking about other people. Like your mom and your sister. That's the way you were raised."

I gritted my teeth. My dad knew how much I did for my mom and sister. But I refused to let him rile me. "I'll get to it soon," I told him. "You know I always put the tree together right after Allison goes to sleep."

"You'll get to it now."

I sighed. There was no use trying to make my case to a man desperate to prove he still had some authority in a house where he no longer lived. So I set down my guitar and rolled out of bed.

In my head, I was already counting down the hours until Christmas was done and I could get back to making music with Jessa Warlow. Until I could lie beside her in the warm golden refuge that was her bedroom.

~ ~ ~

The dreaded holiday began at the asscrack of dawn. It also began in its usual way. With Allison tearing around the house at first light, rousing everyone from Yuletide slumber.

"Lawson! You're not going to hate Christmas this year," she swore when it was my turn to be dragged bodily from bed. Her eyes were wild. Her hair in early morning disarray. "Not after you see what I got you."

I doubted that very much, but I was glad Allison was still able to muster that little kid kind of joy over Christmas. She wasn't exactly mature for a girl who had just turned sixteen and signed up for her learner's permit, but I wouldn't have had it any other way. I didn't want my sister to grow up any faster than she had to.

By the time I pulled on some clothes and made my weary way upstairs, my parents were already lingering in the kitchen, waiting for the coffee to brew. My dad was a lifelong early riser, but seeing my mom awake before noon was a Christmas miracle in itself. Even more miraculous, she had also made some efforts she didn't usually bother with, such as running a comb through her long hair and layering a fresh terrycloth bathrobe over her nightgown. Her eyes—the same bright blue as mine and Thom's—sparkled behind her glasses.

When my mother went to my father, I turned away. Seeing her acting girlish and smitten over a man who had (for all intents and purposes) left her was just too much. Eyes averted, I joined Alli in the living room, where she was already inspecting the pile of gifts under the tree.

As soon as my jeans touched the carpet, she pushed a neatly-wrapped gift in my direction. "I know you're going to like this one. And not in the way where you pretend to like something so I don't get my feelings hurt."

I shook the box gently. "You didn't have to do this."

"You sure didn't," I heard my dad mutter as he and my mother settled onto our overstuffed living room couch.

If Allison heard him, she didn't let on. "Go on! Open it."

I peeled away the blue paper, and opened up a medium-sized box packed with peanuts. Then I sucked in air.

"Alli. How did you even know what to buy?" I reached in and lifted out a pair of serious, high-quality headphones. The kind you might find in a recording studio.

"Kate's mom took us to Philadelphia to shop, and I asked at the store. Are they the right kind?"

I turned them over in my hands. "They're perfect. Thank you, Allison." Usually, my sister gave me gifts that were meaningful, but inexpensive. Even handmade. This time, she had gone overboard. Of course, I kept my mouth shut. Allison waited for Christmas all year, and I wouldn't have ruined it for the world.

My dad, however, wasn't one to hold his tongue. "Where did you get the money for something like that, Allison?"

"Let's not talk about money." She was already digging back through her gifts, organizing her booty and setting aside her favorites. "Let's talk about presents!"

My father was not to be put off so easily. "You had to have used your birthday money, Allison. The money from me." His neck burned a furious red.

Allison pulled on a new puffer jacket and slipped her feet into a pair of fur-lined slippers. "I used some of my birthday money," she said absently. "So what?"

"So that's not what I sent it for. I sent it for you to use on yourself. For school clothes, and doing fun things with your friends."

"Lawson gives me spending money all year. I don't want to buy him something with his own money. That would be so tacky."

My father's face hardened and he put out his hand. "Give me those headphones."

"Why?"

"Just give them here. Do you have the receipt?"

"Well . . . yes," Allison answered slowly. "It's in the box." She didn't get his gist just yet. Not completely.

"Okay. Give me the box too."

With a little gasp, Allison understood. "I don't want to." Her hazel eyes filmed over with tears, but she handed over the box anyway.

I stared at my father. I had been working hard not to take his bait, not to let him get to me. But he'd gone too far. "Those are my things," I told him quietly. "Just put them aside and we'll talk about this later."

My father's eyes shifted my way. "So you're giving me orders now, in my house. It's almost like you're getting the idea that you're in charge around here."

"I hardly think you are," I blurted out.

My dad's eyes lit up like he'd just won a lottery. "Say that again," he urged, all too happy to avail himself of those old fighting words.

I got to my feet, but my father got to his faster. I guess he thought we were going to tangle right there in the middle of the living room, the way he and Thom used to.

But I had no intention of taking a swing at my father— or receiving one either. Instead, I stepped around him. That threw him off and sent him stumbling.

"Where are you going?" he demanded.

"I'm leaving." I grabbed my keys, which were splayed out on the kitchen counter.

"You'll do no such thing," my father snapped. But all the pep had gone out of his step. "Sit your butt back down right now," he tried. "You're going to upset your mother."

When I glanced in my mother's direction, she stared into her coffee mug as if there was some sort of fascinating message in the sludge at the bottom of her cup. She wouldn't say a word in my defense. She never did.

I didn't dare meet Alli's eyes. I knew she'd only burst into tears. So I zipped up my sweatshirt, pulled up my hood, and got the hell out of there.

While I sat shivering in the Nissan, I wished hard that I could understand what had happened to my dad since the days when my parents met each other. In my mom's old pictures, my dad is always somewhere in the background, looking standoffish and dreamy instead of bitter and impatient. If he wasn't playing his guitar, it was strapped to his back. Whatever had happened to that guy, I wasn't sure. I only knew he was long gone.

Anyway, there was no use sitting around cursing my father and listening to my own teeth chatter. I needed somewhere to *go*. Matt's house wasn't an option. Ever since I'd backed out of our university plans, we'd been avoiding each other in a way that we both pretended was accidental, but was very much on purpose. There were a few guys from work I considered calling up, but we were only on-the-clock friends—if that—and I knew it.

After a few more vain attempts at a crackerjack idea about where to park my bones on Christmas Day, I began thinking a thought I had been trying hard not think. Then considering something I had been trying hard not to consider. That something was, of course, a trip to Jessa's house.

As badly as I wanted to see her, I wasn't keen on the idea of showing up on her doorstep like a baby or a puppy that nobody wants. But I was desperate and freezing. And being alone on Christmas, well . . . that's the kind of thing that can break a guy.

Chapter 4

Outside the Warlow home, I paced nervously on the front porch. In my mind's eye, I saw Jessa throwing open the door and regarding me with mild annoyance, or (worse) pity, and that was enough to make me want to turn and run. As the door creaked open, I almost did. But when I pried my gaze off the concrete, I didn't see Jessa at all.

Instead, Mrs. Warlow stood before me, squinting with eyes much like her daughter's, but in a frostier shade of green. "Can I help you?"

"I'm a friend of Jessa's," I explained quickly. "We write music together."

Mrs. Warlow's icy aspect melted all at once. "Ah, yes." The corners of her mouth lifted. "We're so glad Jessa's concentrating on her music again. You'll find her in her room."

"Thank you," I said, peering inside. At the end of the hallway, Jessa's father worked at a laptop at the kitchen table in his slippers. I couldn't see any decorations. "And, uh, merry Christmas."

Jessa was indeed in her bedroom. Once upstairs, I lingered in Jessa's doorway, watching her play a guitar I didn't recognize.

If she was surprised to see me, she didn't show it. "Oh, hi," she said when she finally spotted me. Like it was any other day.

"Hi," I said shortly. I nodded my head at the unfamiliar instrument in her hands. "Gift?"

"Why, yes it is. Trouble is, I thought I'd sound amazing on this horribly expensive guitar. Instead I sound like cats dying and mating."

I shrugged. "You'll get used to it. The action is a little lower than on your Crafter. Give it a couple of hours and you should find it's actually easier for you."

Jessa looked at me with what I liked to imagine was appreciation. "Well, all right, Lawson. I'll keep the faith." She patted the yellow shag carpet in front of her, inviting me to sit down. "Want to play for a while?"

"Why not?" I sank down to the floor and reached for Jessa's Taylor.

"Why don't we try something new?" she suggested. "New music, new lyrics, everything."

"I'm not sure. I wouldn't know where to start."

Jessa reached under her bed and grabbed her notebook. "We'll make it easy. Give me a riff, and I'll see if any of my lyrics are a fit."

"Okay. I can handle that." I had been toying with a simple lead on Christmas Eve—before my father interrupted me. I played it a few times.

"I like it," Jessa declared as I played it a few times more.

At first, she hummed along. Then she broke from my melody line so she could try one of her own. She didn't even have to glance at her notebook—the words just seemed to come to her.

Without thinking, I moved to a more open, ringing part.

Jessa sat up excitedly. "I think you just wrote our chorus, Lawson. Let's try it again. I want to record it on my phone this time so we don't forget."

There were a lot of stops, re-starts, and discussions as we built our song from the ground up. The work was absorbing. More of a challenge, mentally, than expanding on a song that already existed. I was glad for that—it kept me from thinking. But, eventually, I couldn't turn my head off. I mean, at some point, Jessa and I were going to have an uncomfortable conversation about how long it would be appropriate to stay—and just how irritated her mother would be if I was there at dinnertime.

I put down my guitar mid-verse.

"Hey!" Jessa protested. "Why'd you stop?"

I picked at the bottom of my jeans. "I'm interrupting you today, aren't I? I'm interrupting you and your family."

She scoffed. "Interrupting what? My mother made some really dry scones for breakfast and my father gave me a gift I already picked out at the store."

"What about Christmas dinner?" I challenged.

"Around here, we leave it at breakfast. My dad's working on a paper. I think my mother started the laundry. And here I am, with you, trying to write a record. I think it's going pretty well, too. That song we just came up with is going to be our best. I can already tell."

"Really?" I warmed with what felt like a compliment. "Then let's keep going. I won't interrupt again. I promise."

But Jessa had already set her guitar back on its stand. "First, I think you should tell me what's wrong. And what you're really doing here."

"What do you mean?"

"I mean, why aren't you at home, spending Christmas with your family?"

I hesitated. I wasn't sure how much I wanted to admit, or how much Jessa really wanted to know. I considered telling her that my family "left it at breakfast" too, but I had never been a convincing liar.

"My dad was trying to pick a fight," I said finally, "and I didn't want to be in one."

Jessa cocked her chin. "Why on earth would he do that?"

I wasn't sure I had arrived at a complete answer to that question. Still, the words came spilling out. "The way my mom relies on me—and how attached my sister is to me—I think it makes him jealous." I felt my blood pressure rising. "I don't know what he expects. I mean, I'm the one that takes care of them when he won't."

"What do you mean when you say take care of them?"

"Of course there's more to it, like just being there and helping Allison with her homework, but I mean bills mostly. My dad doesn't send my mom any money, and she hasn't had anything from her publisher for almost a year."

"So what are you living on?"

"What I make as a cook."

Jessa was unable to hide her surprise. "All three of you?"

I turned away. "Hey, forget it."

Jessa reached for my hand, but I pulled it back.

"I'm sorry," she said. "I didn't mean to get too personal."

I felt very strange. Sort of exposed. "Today was a terrible mistake," I said, without really meaning to. "I shouldn't have come here. It's Christmas. It's a major holiday." I was just thinking out loud, but for some reason I couldn't shut up. "I'm just your guitarist—*songwriting partner*, if you want to be really generous—and I still show up on your doorstep unannounced. Then I tell you all my problems like some angst-ridden teenager."

"You can come over here whenever you want," Jessa insisted. "On holidays, major and minor, and you can talk to me. About anything you want to."

"You don't have to say that."

Jessa made another grab for my hand. Her fingers wound through mine. "I said it because I like you! I mean, I really fucking like you. You're smart, and very easy to be with. I wouldn't want to sit around my bedroom for hours at a time with just anybody. No matter how good they were on the guitar."

I fidgeted.

She narrowed her eyes. "We're just getting to know each other and all, but I see good things coming, Lawson Harper."

I almost didn't believe her. I hadn't dared hope that Jessa Warlow would actually be into me.

But there it was. She'd said it, clear as anything. Jessa "saw good things." I was suddenly fighting a smile. Then a grin. Finally, I just gave in. Messed-up mouth be damned.

Chapter 5

It was crazy. Unbelievable. For me, there had never been a toy in the bottom of the battered cereal box that was life. Anything I wanted, I had to earn. There were no extras, no bonuses, no pleasant surprises. And yet, with Jessa all I'd had to do was be myself. Somehow, that was enough.

Even my brother's impending arrival didn't trouble me. Jessa and I had already decided. We would just keep quiet about our musical partnership—and the other things going on between us—for a little while. We didn't know exactly what Thom's return would look like, but we knew he wouldn't come quietly. It was no time to make any big announcements.

As for Thom, no one was sure exactly when he would show. He gave no ETA, and it was impossible to keep track of his halting, serpentine progress across the country. One night, my brother would forgo sleep and plow through three states without stopping. The next, he would check in at a hotel and we wouldn't hear from him for two days. I hoped like hell that didn't mean drugs. I couldn't bear the idea of drugs coming into our house while Allison was living at home.

One gray, drizzling evening in the early part of February, Thom simply appeared. Allison and I were hunched over our homework at the kitchen table when the distinctive thud of a slammed trunk made us both jump to attention. Then there was the sound of a key jingling in the lock. Then there was Thom.

He materialized at the shadowy entrance to the kitchen, a duffel bag slung over one shoulder.

Suddenly a little kid again, Allison ran to him and hurled herself into his arms.

"Little sister!" Laughing, Thom staggered backward. "Well, you've certainly grown."

With some effort, he set Allison back down on the linoleum. He tugged at her hair. "I guess you're a young woman now, eh, Goldilocks?"

Alli beamed.

Thom turned his gaze to me. "And you, Lawson! I can hardly call you 'kid brother.' You're not a kid anymore."

I could only stare. Thom looked incredibly different from the last time I'd seen him in person. He was only twenty-five, but he appeared weathered. Probably from sun and surf and occasional hard living. His face was bony and rough, and his hair was bleached almost white. Those eyes of his were exactly the same, though. Bright blue and twinkling with some permanent amusement. They would probably stay that way till he was a hundred.

Before I could come up with something to say to the brother I hadn't laid eyes on in four years, my mother came hustling into the kitchen, nightgown swirling around her heels. "Oh, Thom." She squeezed his sinewy form to her plump one. "You're really home!"

"You don't know how good it feels." He sighed. "I've put off this trip far too long." Then, like it was no big deal, Thom lit a cigarette.

Not a single cigarette had been smoked in the confines of our home since Thom moved away. The smell of tobacco, mixed with our usual house smell, was strange and unsettling.

~ ~ ~

In the morning, when I meandered into the kitchen, there was Thom at the kitchen table, hunched over his coffee.

"Still an early riser," he said. "You always were."

I grabbed my mother's old Garfield mug and poured myself a generous cup of my brother's brew. There was plenty in the pot. "You weren't."

He shrugged. "I guess you and Allison aren't the only ones who've changed."

I stared at Thom as he sipped his coffee with one hand and rolled a cigarette with the other. Whether he rolled his cigarettes because he couldn't afford a pack of smokes or because he deemed it the more stylish choice, I didn't know.

"So tell me, brother, what are you doing with that musical talent of yours?"

I couldn't remember my brother ever asking me about myself. I wondered if maybe he really had changed in some significant way.

"I recently connected with a songwriter," I explained, careful not to sound evasive—or give too much away. "Somebody local. We've written enough songs for a set. Or an album. Eventually, we'll record them all."

Thom pounded on the table. "Well good for you. I know Dad thinks you simply must go to college lest you become a degenerate like yours truly. But you know he's become a philistine in his middle age. I say, take a chance on your art."

Without missing a beat, Thom lit up a fresh roll-your-own. "You know what I think? I think, when I go back to Los Angeles, you should come with me."

"I don't know, Thom. I think L.A. is more your kind of place."

He shrugged. "Hey, I know L.A. gets a bad rap. People think it's all glamour and fast living. That's just what they show on TV. There's all kinds of jobs in the music industry, and lots of hard-working people who do them. I have many friends who work at the labels and studios—behind the scenes."

"Okay. I guess I never thought about it that way." I hadn't. And maybe, if the last three months of my life had gone differently, I would have considered my brother's invitation. Of course, things being as they were, I had no plans to go anywhere that didn't have Jessa Warlow in it.

"One more thing," my brother went on. "I'm having a get-together tonight. Just a small gathering with a few of my old friends. Ronnie Bianchi—remember her?—is spreading the word. Anyway, I'd like for you to be there."

"Well, I live here, Thom. I guess I have to be."

"Ha! Right. You know what I mean. I want you to be part of things. Not like when you and Allison were kids, hiding in your bedrooms."

"All right, Thom," I agreed. I stood and downed the rest of my coffee. "I'll come straight home after work. I guess I'll see you then. I have to get to class."

That was true. I also wanted to avail myself of Allison's phone. Before I left for the community college, I wanted to send Jessa a message with the big news. That Thom was in town, and he was already planning a "small gathering." Of course, if my suspicions were correct, there would be nothing small about it.

~ ~ ~

When I turned onto my street after my shift at Ralphie's, cars lined the curb on both sides of the road and all the lights in the house were burning. The distinct thud of bass rattled my car windows from two blocks away.

A couple of cars were tandem parked on the left side of the driveway, so I took the spot directly behind my mother's wood-paneled station wagon. As soon as I got out, I could hear the buzz of conversation and sharp laughter. The thrash of seventies rock. When I reached the porch, I hung back for a minute or two, just to get myself mentally prepared. Then I took a deep breath, pulled up my hood, and let myself inside.

At once, I was struck by the way my house seemed to have grown. You'd think that packing a tiny place far past the fire department's approved capacity would shrink it, but not so. My shoebox of a house had morphed into a never-ending labyrinth, with something or someone to be seen in even the most forgotten corners.

A few girls I recognized vaguely from Thom's high school days talked in hushed voices by the coat closet. More heads gathered in the kitchen, which was noisy with chatter and the sound of feet squelching on the linoleum. When I peered down the hallway, I saw an actual line for the bathroom, like you'd see at a nightclub.

I was certainly eager to explore the rest of the grounds. But first, I wanted to make sure my mother was okay.

I dodged bodies all the way down the hallway, then gave her door a good, hard knock. "It's me. Lawson," I said, just loudly enough to be heard above the din.

"Come in!" my mother sang.

"How are you?" I asked as I closed the door behind me.

My mother was sitting up in bed, laptop on her knees. Her eyes, as always, were large and childlike. "Just fine, Lawson." She lifted her gaze ceilingward as if savoring the noise and chaos. As if they were somehow holy in whatever alternate universe my mother inhabited. "This house has been much too quiet for much too long."

I knew that was a subtle dig at me, and maybe Allison, but I decided to ignore it. I also didn't bother to ask my mother if she was working on her latest novel. I knew she wasn't. When I was a kid, she turned out two or three a year—mostly books about fairies and fauns fucking each other and that kind of thing. I couldn't say exactly what had happened since then, but every year it was more of a struggle to get my mom behind her typewriter. Or do any of those annoying tasks expected of a responsible adult, like paying bills or keeping track of Allison. Speaking of which . . .

"Alli at Kate's?" I asked.

My mother settled into her pillows. "Of course. You know Miss Priss won't have her little friends over here. I'm so glad Thom's not ashamed to have anybody by." She regarded me pointedly. "I hope you're not getting snobbish like Allison, Lawson. I haven't seen Matthew around here lately."

I didn't want to admit that my old buddy Matt and I hadn't been associating much since I'd put the kibosh on our college plans. "I've been busy," I said instead.

"Of course. I know how much you love to work."

I cringed. I hated it when my mother pretended I worked for pure enjoyment. That I took all the overtime I could get because it was some kind of thrill. But I didn't let on. There was a time when I tried to reason with my mother. To get through to her. It never did any good.

I got up. "I should go back out there," I said. "You know, to keep an eye on things."

"Yes," my mother said, "make sure we don't run out of pop or booze, and make sure the party doesn't get *dull*."

I nodded. "Right." If my mother didn't care if anybody threw up in the sink or put holes in the wall, I guess I didn't either. With a sigh, I let myself out into the hallway.

As I moved through the house, I kept my hood halfway down over my eyes. That allowed me to observe uninterrupted, and to listen, incognito, to conversations that weren't meant for my ears.

A group stationed near the refrigerator recounted stories about Thom's years in California—none of them true. One guy heard Thom was working as a model. A second that he'd become an ascetic monk in a remote beachfront community. Another that Thom had been selling his body on Santa Monica Boulevard until he hit it big day-trading.

I didn't bother to offer corrections. I just snickered and kept moving. There was more to see.

In the living room, Thom himself held court from his royal position in the easy chair. He was regaling the crowd on the couch and on the floor around the coffee table with the tale of his cross-country journey.

I didn't stop. I wasn't interested in hearing about Thom's potentially drug-addled adventures.

I ducked, ready to slip past the couch and out the sliding doors. But when I took one last glance behind me, I saw something that stopped me in my tracks. Standing uncertainly at the entrance to the kitchen about twenty feet away was . . . Jessa. She had obviously walked from her place. Her hair was windblown and her cheeks were pink. Her eyes, damp and a little bloodshot, were intensely green.

A weird little ache worked its way up my spine. It was incredibly strange knowing Jessa had come at someone else's invitation, with the intention of spending time with people who were not me. I had to fight the urge to go to her, but I didn't have to fight the urge for long.

The second one old friend spotted her and called her name, Jessa was surrounded. Partygoers flanked her on each side and peppered her with questions. Someone pushed a beer into her hand. I couldn't have reached her if I tried.

Over the tops of the many heads between us, I watched Jessa's reaction. Panic flickered over her face. She'd been anxious about admitting to her friends that she quit her job and moved back in with her parents. If she'd hoped to ease into it—well, no dice. But then, very quickly, Jessa's aspect changed. She raised her head and pressed her shoulders back.

"I'm here in Gunther to write music," I heard her explain coolly. "I'll be sure to let you know about any further developments."

~ ~ ~

The rest of the evening passed with incredible speed. When I ran into Thom's ex Lindsay in the kitchen, she demanded to know everything I'd been doing in the last few years—and I obliged. Our neighbor Benji wanted to have a beer out back. Ronnie, who had been part of Thom's tight-knit high school crew, greeted me with a whoop.

"Look at that. It's little Law Harper all grown up!" she exclaimed. Then she dragged me into Thom's bedroom, where her best friend Joe had set up a portable stereo. "You're a musician," she said. "You know music, and Thom said you've got all your Dad's old tapes and CDs. Help us DJ."

Joe, a gentle giant with the same sideburns he'd worn in high school, passed me a bottle of beer. It wasn't the cheap stuff that other guests had socked away in the fridge. "We've got a stash going," he said. "For the inner circle."

"Am I *in* the inner circle?"

"Of course you are." Ronnie threw an arm around my shoulders. "You're a Harper."

For hours, Joe, Ronnie, and I sipped beers and selected from the stacks of CDs and cassette tapes I hauled up from the basement. I was having such a good time that I forgot to wonder what Jessa was doing. Before I knew it, the wee hours had arrived. Ronnie and Joe left for their place in Conshohocken—and I put myself on cleanup duty.

I grabbed a garbage bag and went outside to empty the cereal bowls and coffee mugs that had been co-opted as ashtrays. Then I headed back inside to gather up the bottles and cans that had been abandoned on every available surface. The work was soothing—even hypnotic. But just when I started to really zone out, a hand clapped me on the back. When I whipped around, I found Thom wearing one of his Cheshire cat grins.

"Lawson! Are you really cleaning?" He seized the garbage bag and shoved it behind him. "I won't have it. You're supposed to be enjoying yourself."

"I did enjoy myself tonight," I told him honestly.

"Glad to hear it, little brother. Anyway, I do have a favor to ask of you. One that I don't think you'll find entirely unpleasant."

"What kind of favor?"

"Well." Thom paused. "You remember Jessa Warlow, don't you?"

I blinked. "Yes. Of course."

"I thought so! Would you be a gentleman and walk her home? I won't hear of her going out alone at this hour, when there might be lunatics about."

Very suddenly, Jessa was at Thom's side. Her eyes were dancing. "Sorry to trouble you, Lawson," she said smoothly. "I could hardly ask Thom to leave his own party. I thought perhaps his little brother might have a few moments to spare."

"Sure, it's no problem," I told her just as smoothly. Obviously, Jessa had suggested I accompany her home. I could hardly believe she'd dared. "Just let me get my jacket."

Chapter 6

"Well, that went rather swimmingly," Jessa said as we disappeared into the darkness of the trees.

The pines rose up around us, tall and fragrant. A lopsided gibbous moon lit our way. She took my hand. "I think we've managed to steal a few moments together."

I smiled. A few hours before, I was struck by the fear that I might lose Jessa to her many friends and admirers. But she hadn't forgotten me. Quite to the contrary, Jessa had concocted a story so she could see me alone.

I suddenly felt very brave. Even a little bit reckless. "What if we could be alone tonight? I mean, all night?"

Jessa laughed. "But how?"

I stopped. "Follow me." Without another word, I turned on my heels and began moving at a fast clip back toward the house.

"Lawson!" Jessa called. "Where are you going? Someone will see you!"

To my right, a few partygoers lingered on the lawn. The dancing shadows, much larger than life, gave the impression that they were many. Their voices, amplified against the side of the house, made them seem only steps away. But all of that was mere illusion. I had played hide-and-seek in my backyard thousands of times. I knew no one could see me in the thickest part of the trees.

Finally, I heard Jessa sigh. Then there was the soft sound of twigs snapping underfoot as she hustled to catch up.

By the time Jessa reached my side, we were standing

at the top of the six concrete steps on the north side of the house.

"Oh," Jessa whispered, as she peered down at the basement door. "Your room?" One eyebrow arched beautifully. "Darling, I didn't know you had such a sense of adventure."

Nor, I guess, did I. But when it came to Jessa Warlow, I was willing to toss any number of rules out the window.

We took all six steps together. At the bottom, I unlocked the door quietly as a cat burglar, then listened nervously. The slurry conversations went on and the elongated shadows continued their strange dance. We were home free.

I felt around for the light switch, flicked it, and all at once my bedroom was flooded with the shadowy kind of light that only exists in basements.

Jessa ducked under my arm. That's when I discovered her to be the only person in the history of the world who is even more striking under an exposed bulb. She circled in front of me and turned, taking in her surroundings. The weak yellow light caught the gold in her hair and flecks of bronze I didn't even know existed in her irises, which had always appeared so solidly, certainly green.

I watched Jessa wander over to the bed for closer inspection. She ran her hands over the orange comforter. Then she let herself fall onto the bed, and made snow angels in the thick down.

Smiling big, I crossed the basement and flopped down beside her. We leaned into each other, our knees drawn up and our hands linked together. All the while, the ceiling groaned and heaved above us and the stomping of feet echoed through the basement.

There was something magical about being alone together, in our own private place, while the party went on over our heads. I guess Jessa felt it too, because she rolled on top of me and pressed her lips against my neck. I gasped as the heat rolled through me, making me a human fireball. Then my voice, involuntarily, was speaking into the semi-darkness.

"Jessa," I said, "I think I'm going to fall in love with you."

She laughed. "Are you asking if that's okay with me?"

"Yes. I guess I am."

Jessa flashed her most wicked smile, narrowing her eyes in that catlike way of hers. "Well, you just go right ahead, Lawson Harper."

Under that thick down comforter, our bodies were a line of unbroken heat. The cold, damp air of the basement was a distant memory. When the party ceased to exist, I couldn't say. I couldn't even tell you the exact moment when I went to sleep. I just know that in the morning, Jessa and I woke in a tangle of limbs, with the blankets pulled entirely over our heads.

When we threw off the covers, the sun was already pouring through the slats in the small windows at the top of the cinderblock walls. It was tempting to stay right there and stage a lie-in until I had to leave for work, but we didn't want to tempt fate. So Jessa dressed and kissed me on the mouth. Then she was slipping out the basement door.

The sliver of light from outside caught her hair and illuminated the green of her eyes, seemingly from behind. She waved goodbye and then she, and that piercing slice of light, were gone.

I remained curled up in bed, starry-eyed and woozy, for what felt like a very long time. Then, finally, I stumbled upstairs.

In the kitchen, there was Thom, nursing a cup of coffee and staring into space. The brilliant morning sunlight bisected his face, making one blue eye appear overexposed. "Hey, Law," he said.

I jumped.

He didn't notice. "Thanks for escorting Jessa last night. Can you believe she wanted to go home all alone at two a.m.? Stubborn, isn't she?"

"Incorrigible."

"Ha." Thom turned to me, his eyes suddenly coming into focus. "That dry sense of humor catches me off guard every time." He squinted.

"You know, I'm sorry I never really got to know you, Lawson. I guess it was the age difference. And just me being a self-centered asshole, of course. This time, though, things are going to be different between us. No kidding!"

Chapter 7

After work, I came home to find Thom waiting at the door with my falling-apart corduroy jacket.

"No party tonight?"

Thom shook his head. "It's Lindsay's birthday, and I've received word that she's hosting a 'girls' night out' at McGuillicutti's." His smile twisted into a grin. "Let's crash it."

"All right," I agreed. Lindsay wasn't the type of girl who would mind being "crashed." Anyway, I had a hunch that Jessa would be in attendance at Lindsay's gathering. The two of them had never been best friends, but they were part of the same group of friends. That, I figured, counted for something.

And so Thom and I headed out into the cool night. We walked briskly up Broad, hung a left at Main, then crossed the street to McGuillicutti's.

As expected, the place was packed. During the week, McGuillicutti's is a locals-only spot reserved for old timers and career alcoholics. Friday and Saturday nights are a different story. Mostly due to a lack of better options, young Gunther comes out in droves to dirty dance while imbibing as many hurriedly prepared cocktails as possible.

Lindsay spotted Thom and I almost as soon as we got in the door. After wagging her finger in our direction, she bounded over and straightened her pink cowboy hat, which someone had adorned with a glittery *25*.

"Here on girls' night? Naughty, naughty!" she

admonished. But she was grinning. Then she was dragging us into the fray.

Thom and I were quickly separated as female forms moved wildly around us, waving their hands and whooping along with the music. One particularly intoxicated young lady danced theatrically in front of Thom while a tall brunette stepped into grinding position.

He pretended to be flattered, but I knew Thom was just humoring Lindsay's friends. He had always dealt strictly in women who wouldn't be out of place on a billboard or in a magazine.

When one of Lindsay's minions grabbed for me, I dodged. I wanted to look for Jessa. I didn't know if she would be in attendance—but I hoped so. Since I'd taken on the "chore" of walking her home after Thom's party, I knew nobody would think twice if we said hello.

I pushed through the crowd, searching for a flash of mossy eyes or tawny hair. Near the edge of the dance floor, I noticed a few girls from Thom's circle, including Ronnie, holding aloft shot glasses. I elbowed in their direction. When Ronnie stepped back and downed 1.5 fluid ounces of something oversweet and sticky, she revealed a lovely sight. Jessa, in a strappy dress. Sipping a gin and tonic.

I squeezed in next to her and put a hand to the small of her back.

Instantly, Jessa broke into a smile. "Lawson! How bold of you to show up uninvited."

"That's my favorite way to show up. Didn't you know?"

Jessa laughed. "I'll come see you in the morning," she said near my ear. "Soon as I wake up."

"Can't wait," I told her.

Now that I had Jessa so near, it would be hell to pull myself away. I summoned all of my willpower. But, as it turned out, my efforts were unnecessary. Because Ronnie cut in. "My turn!"

She stumbled into me and grabbed my shoulders. Her beer spilled down the back of my hoodie in a cold trickle.

"Hey, Ronnie," I said as I swiped her pint and set it down on the nearest bar table. "Why don't we get you something else to drink? Maybe a cola."

"Hey, Lawson," she slurred. "Call me when you're twenty-five." She pinned me against said table, moving in a loose approximation of dancing.

Over Ronnie's head, I locked eyes with Jessa, who regarded me with both surprise and amusement. It seemed neither of us had ever seen Ronnie so drunk.

Just as Ronnie lunged, attempting to plant a kiss on my lips, I felt someone collect a fistful of my hoodie and yank me away.

It was Thom. He laughed and shook his head. Then he toted me right out of the bar.

Out on the street, I sucked cold, fresh air into my lungs. It was heavenly, after breathing in the bar's dense atmosphere.

My brother, obviously less concerned with air quality, lit one of his tightly-rolled cigarettes. "Time to ride into the sunset," he drawled.

So, that was it. We had crashed the party and slipped away before any of the girls even noticed we were missing. There was something thrilling about it all. I had to admit. When it came to having a good time, my brother knew what he was doing.

While we trudged down Gunther's cracked sidewalks, Thom puffed away contentedly. "Glad I pried you out of Ronnie's lovestruck grip?"

"Ah, yes. Thanks for that."

"I knew one of my friends would end up with a crush on my little brother! Ronnie's cute, but I figure it's time we got you a really *pretty* girlfriend, Law. I mean, I know you're into the quiet, studious thing. But, still . . . you're a Harper!"

"I don't have any problem with how Ronnie looks, Thom. It's just that, to me, she's a friend—and that's all. Anyway, I don't think Ronnie's really interested. She was wasted. I guess it was all those birthday shots."

Thom snickered. "You know what? All the girls have been raving about Ronnie's short hair, but I think it makes her a little chipmunk-y. Why do women do that? Encourage each other to get unflattering haircuts, I mean. Is it a primal urge to reduce competition for mating opportunities?"

"Well, jeez, Thom. I wouldn't know." I wasn't interested in dissecting the appearances of the women of Gunther. It seemed mean-spirited.

Thom went on anyway. "Then there's Lindsay. Good thing I broke it off with her after graduation. She's still got legs a mile long, but can you believe all the makeup she piles on? I guess she thinks we can't tell she's starting to look like her mother under that mask."

"That's not very nice." I liked Lindsay. She could be loud, but she was a good sport through all of Thom's high school shenanigans. Also, she was the only one of Thom's high school friends who really paid attention to me and Allison when we were little kids. Hell, she even babysat us a couple of times.

All the way home, Thom went on smoking and smiling to himself. I tried to enjoy the crisp air and the silence. Then I got to wondering what Thom would have to say about Jessa. She was part of the old gang, and she had been there at McGuillicutti's too.

I waited for my brother to pick up where he left off, but he stayed mum when we hung a left into our driveway, and when we strolled past my mother's station wagon, and when we ambled up the path and onto the porch.

While Thom unlocked the door, I watched a bunch of moths fry themselves on the yellow porch light. Then I piped up. I almost couldn't help it.

"Well," I said, in my most casual voice, "what do you think about Jessa Warlow?"

Thom raised his eyebrows high, then pushed open the door. As he traversed the foyer, he chuckled to himself. I followed him into the living room, where he flopped onto the couch and crossed his Pumas on the coffee table.

"Ha!" he said finally. "Do you even have to ask? Those cat's eyes would drive anybody mad. But who even cares about that? Jessa's beyond such petty analysis. She struts around like a fucking queen because she is one."

I could add to that. I could add to that for miles. Jessa was irresistible because she comported herself like a lady, but if you looked in her eyes, you could see she was really fearless and somewhat savage. And even when she was perfectly still, she was really tingling with some new ambition. Of course I couldn't say any of that to Thom.

"I don't agree," I lied. "She's pretty—but nothing special."

Thom dropped his cigarette in astonishment. "Well, shit. To each his own, I guess!" He rolled over and picked up the still-burning butt, but it was too late. It had already singed a little hole in the rug.

"Anyway . . ." He produced a fresh cigarette from the pack in his coat pocket. "Everybody thinks it's adorable that you and Jessa are buddies now. Ever since I put you on walking-home duty." Thom lit up. "So tell me," he said, his voice suddenly husky, "when you were alone with her, did she say anything about me?"

"Anything like what?"

Thom shrugged bashfully. It was strange to see him acting that way, when he was usually so smug and sure of himself.

"Ah. Never mind. I was just trying to get a read on things."

"What things?"

"Come on, Law. Catch up. I'm telling you that I'm into Jessa. I mean, really into her. You asked me why I came here, to Gunther. I heard Jessa was in town. Our old friend Benji saw her a few times, driving her parents' car."

Thom's words functioned like a jab to the spleen. I sat down hard in the easy chair parked conveniently behind me. "But, Thom. You knew her all that time in high school, and you were never interested."

"Wasn't *interested?*" He snorted. "Hardly. I just understood I didn't have a shot. I mean, I knew full well she didn't take me seriously. How could she? I was a joker. I was all over the place. I was always breaking up with Lindsay to chase the next girl in my line of vision. This time, I'm focused. Jessa's the only one I want, and I'm going to let her know it."

Thom settled back into the couch. "You're awfully quiet over there, Lawson. Did I take you by surprise?"

That, of course, was the understatement of the century. It had never occurred to me that Thom might be into Jessa. Or that he would come all the way to Gunther in search of some misguided happily ever after. I had to tell him about me and Jessa, and I had to do it quickly.

Thom leaned forward. "What is it? Is Jessa seeing someone?"

I coughed. "It's actually . . ." I began, "I mean, it's really kind of funny." I reneged. "All right. It's not funny at all."

My brother stared at me like I belonged in the nuthouse. "What's got into you, Law? You're acting pretty weird, you know."

I did know. I tried my best to collect myself and behave like a human. "There's something I haven't told you. Remember I said I was writing music?"

"Of course."

"I mean, I said I was writing music with a partner. A local songwriter."

"Yes. Go on." Thom gestured for me to hurry.

"That local songwriter is Jessa, Thom. She asked me to collaborate right after she moved in with her parents."

"Ha!" Thom grinned. "I had no idea."

"No one did. I mean, no one does. Our songs are still in the works. They're not ready to show to the world. Or anybody at all, as a matter of fact."

"Well, isn't that just too perfect? I look forward to hearing these songs of yours."

"Sure. You'll be the first. I mean, if you want to be." I swallowed. "That's not everything, though."

"What is it? Did Jessa tell you something at one of your little band practices? I mean, about who she's seeing? It's that guy she was practically engaged to back in Philadelphia, isn't it?"

"No. No, it isn't. Thom, what I'm trying to tell you is, Jessa is seeing *me*."

"I'm not in the mood to joke around right now, Law."

"I'm not making a joke."

"I wish you'd just get to the—"

"Thom," I interrupted, "listen to me. With me and Jessa, it started with the music. Then it was something more. I'm sorry. I didn't know you were into her."

"Jesus." Thom raised up on his elbows and looked me over. "You're not kidding, are you?"

I shook my head. "No."

His eyebrows arched practically to his hairline. "Well, fuck."

"I know," I said. "I didn't believe it at first either. I mean, that she would be interested in me."

Thom blew out a lot of stinking smoke all over the coffee table. "So my kid brother is sleeping with Jessa Warlow."

"I wouldn't say it that way, but . . ." I paused. "You don't hold it against me, do you? I mean, I didn't know how you felt about her. I couldn't have."

Thom chuckled a hollow-sounding chuckle. "No worries, Law. I just learned quite a bit about my baby brother is all."

"What?"

"Apparently, you've got that boy-toy act down pat. I guess I should have known you're not the innocent you pretend to be for mom and Allison's sake. Stupid of me to offer to get you a girlfriend. I know you and that scumbag friend of yours—the Brewer kid—cruise around town at all hours. I'm sure you've had plenty of practice scamming on women."

"Thom. You're not getting me. Not at all. I'm trying to tell you that me and Jessa care about each other. That we're together. You know, like a couple."

Thom put up a hand. "Wait a minute."

"What?"

"You actually think Jessa Warlow is your girlfriend?"

"Of course I do. She is."

He smirked. "Then why hasn't Jessa told anybody about your great romance, Lawson?"

"We were waiting for the right time."

"And when might that be?"

"When we're ready. When our music's ready. When things have settled down."

"That right, little bro?" my brother asked. Then a strange noise originated from somewhere deep within. It sounded like the beginning of a sob, but what emerged was nothing like tears. He was laughing. Big, gut-shaking belly laughs.

"Holy shitballs!" he exclaimed as soon as he could speak. "You're so smart and mature about certain things, Lawson, that sometimes I forget you're practically a child."

"What do you mean?"

Thom put out his cigarette right in the center of the coffee table. "Don't worry about it," he said as he got to his feet. "Have a great night, brother. I'll be spending mine elsewhere."

With that, he shoved his hands in the pockets of his bomber jacket and stepped quickly through the house. And then I heard him slam the front door. And he was gone.

Chapter 8

At nine o'clock in the morning, Jessa showed up at the basement door looking drowsy and beautiful. She had layered her jacket over a simple dress. Her hair, in a braid at her shoulder, was still damp.

"Darling," she said as she nuzzled into me on my bed, "I was glad to see you last night. But much gladder now."

I wanted to lean into her and slip under the covers. To spend the whole morning lost to the world, until I had to peel myself off the sheets and roll into Ralphie's. But I knew I had to tell Jessa what my brother said.

"My brother is in love with you."

She laughed. "What?"

"Really. He told me last night."

"Well, he must have been very drunk. Much like a certain young lady we both know, I suspect."

I shook my head. "He meant it. In fact, that's why he came to Gunther. To be with you."

"Well, don't you worry. I'll set him straight. Thom and I are friends. Nothing more."

"He knows that now. I mean, I told him about you and me right away. I had to."

Jessa cocked her chin. "Wait. What about you and me?"

"Everything. The music. Our . . . you know, our relationship."

"Jesus, Lawson. *Why?*"

Jessa's question threw me. I thought the reasons were obvious, but for some reason, I found myself struggling to explain. "I couldn't leave him in the dark. Let him be a fool.

And meeting you down here . . . the first time, it was all in good fun. If we kept it up, I'd be a liar. A sneak. My brother might never forgive me. He might never forgive either of us."

Jessa drew her knees up and sat next to me in silence for a long time. The pipes gurgled and hissed above us. In the air, the sour tang of mildew mingled with the sweetness of fabric softener.

"Are you okay?" I asked. "Tell me what you're thinking."

Jessa fidgeted. "I'm thinking I'm not ready for this, Lawson. When everybody finds out about us, it's not going to be no big deal. I mean, there's the age difference. And you're Thom's brother. And all of our friends are *around*."

"It's too late," I said gently. "We can't take it back. If everybody talks, they talk. We'll handle the fallout together. Right?"

I smiled, but Jessa didn't smile back.

I reached out my hand, but she didn't take it. Instead, she scooted off the bed. "We can take this back," she said. "I'm sure of it."

"What? How?" I asked, when maybe the real question was *why?*

Let me talk to Thom," Jessa said, pacing, "I'll simply explain to him that we were both very lonely. That we mistook what was a musical connection for a physical one. That it was a mistake. If we're lucky, he won't tell anybody what he knows."

I shook my head. "I don't understand. Why lie when we were going to tell Thom, and everybody, what we are to each other as soon as he left? What's a few weeks, give or take?"

"Lawson. Now, here's the thing . . ." Jessa began. She tried to put her thoughts into words a few more times, but her sentences resisted construction. She started to get a very funny kind of expression on her face.

At first, I didn't know what it meant. Then, very suddenly, I did. "You were never planning to tell anybody about us, were you?" I whispered.

Jessa played with her braid. She wouldn't meet my eye. "Lawson, please."

"Please what?"

"Please don't be angry," she said.

But, of course, it was too late for that. My fists were already shaking at my sides. I stood and pointed toward the door. "Get out."

Jessa's green eyes widened. "What?"

"Get out of my room. Get out of my house." I couldn't believe she thought I had so little self-respect that I would sit around and wait for her to spin some utterly insulting lie for Thom. That I was going to continue on as her slice on the sly. That that would be enough for me. When it wasn't even close.

"Lawson," she said, "you're serious?"

I wasn't sure I could be any more serious. I crossed the basement with big, furious strides and threw open the door. Cold air rushed in, blowing my school papers off the dresser and sending them flying here and there.

Jessa, finally, appeared to get the point. She gathered her jacket around her. "I guess we'll talk about this after you've calmed down."

I couldn't stand to listen to another word. "Go!" I yelled.

She did. Jessa hurried through the basement door, and out of my life.

When she shut the door behind her with a solid bang, I felt somehow satisfied. I was confident that I'd made the right decision. I'd taken a stand. I was in charge of my destiny, and I would not be trifled with.

I marched back toward my bed, shoulders high, head up, and all that. But before I could complete my crossing, pain like I'd never felt ripped through my body. Every organ went into spasms as if something vital had been removed from my system. It hurt so badly I couldn't breathe. Suddenly on the floor, my body quaked from the inside out.

The weight of my pain pinned me to the ground like a concrete slab until, at long last, I found the strength to crawl to my bed. I reached for a pillow and covered my face so I could get myself under control. But there was no control. Everything was finished. Everything I'd believed in so hard. In my future, I'd just seen Jessa. Her body posed on the horizon. My heart hers to have or to destroy. *Destroy*, I thought. She had chosen destroy.

I felt duped. Violated. Thom had known immediately what it took me three months to comprehend. To Jessa, I was an easy friend, a decent guitarist, and I guess a passable lay—but nothing more than that. She was Gunther royalty. I was a twenty-one-year-old cook with a messed-up mouth living in his mother's basement. I knew from the start that I didn't have a real shot with a girl like her. But Jessa had convinced me otherwise. For her own ends . . . she had made me believe.

That thought was what really sent me over the edge. I didn't know where to put all the rage and indignation that was collecting inside me until I found myself knocking over everything in sight. I sent the little nightstand tumbling. I pulled the heavy dresser over. The lamp, the mirror didn't stand a chance. I didn't stop until I had no breath left in my body, and I was just a heap of bones on the mattress.

Seconds later, I heard a frantic knocking on the basement door at the top of the stairs. "Law?" asked a tiny voice. "Are you okay?"

When I lifted my head, I saw a flash of pale hair through the banister. Alli was peering through the railing, master key in hand.

She scurried down the stairs. "It sounded like the whole basement was caving in. What happened?"

"I'm sick."

Allison glanced over the ruins of my room, then regarded me doubtfully. But I meant what I said. I was starting to feel physically ill, with chills and dizziness and everything.

"I'll take care of you!" Allison proclaimed. She helped me upstairs, brought me generous supplies of aspirin and water, and made a nest of blankets on the couch.

I dove right in and drifted into what turned out to be a long, fitful slumber.

Chapter 9

When I finally opened my eyes, the sun had gone down. My blankets were drenched in sweat. My mind was cloudy.

Slowly, I sat up against the back of the couch and waited for my head to clear. Not that I felt any better when it did. Just twenty-four hours ago, I had felt closer to my brother than ever before. I had been looking forward to making a record. I thought I was in love. All that was finished. Yet, somehow, I wasn't destroyed. In fact, I was determined.

There was no denying that I had become the dictionary definition of a loser. Jessa's rejection made that perfectly clear to me, if it wasn't before. But I wasn't going to be a loser much longer. I wouldn't be. I decided then and there. I was going to make my own way in music, without the help of the great Jessa Warlow.

When I glanced up, I saw that Allison was watching me from the kitchen. "What are you thinking?" she asked. "You look so serious."

"I have to find a way to make a career in music," I said. "Or at least give it a try."

Allison crept slowly into the living room and took a seat next to me on the couch. "Lawson, I heard you and Thom talking the night he got here. He said a lot of the music jobs are in L.A."

"Oh, Alli. I didn't know you were listening. I won't go all the way to California. I promise."

"Why not?" She looked me directly in the eye. "I mean, really. Why not?"

"You know Mom can't take care of you, Allison. She can't take care of herself."

"Is that the reason you decided not to go to college with Matt?"

I had said too much. But there was no taking it back. "Yes," I admitted. "I was hoping Mom would get better. She's worse than ever." Alli and I both knew that.

Allison set her chin. "Lawson. I don't know what happened this morning, and I don't know why it's taken you so long to decide to do something with your musical talent. But I do know you can't stay in Gunther for me. Mom isn't okay, but Dad will make sure I am. If I need something—I just have to ask."

I knew, on some level, that was true. My dad wouldn't lift a finger for me, but Allison was a different story. She was a girl—and his favorite. Still, if my dad got involved in Allison's life, he and my mother would have to communicate on a regular basis again. It wouldn't be pretty. It would be tense. Chaotic. All the things I had tried, for so long, to protect Allison from.

"I'm not a little kid anymore," Allison reminded me. "I'm sixteen. I have my learner's permit."

"Of course. I know that." At any other time in my life, I wouldn't have considered leaving Allison alone with my parents and their chaos. But I had never wanted to leave Gunther so badly. I had never wanted to make something of myself so badly.

I wasn't sure I was going to California, or anywhere at all, but I knew what I had to do next. It was time for me, at long last, to talk to Matt.

~ ~ ~

Matt, a future biologist, and I, an English major, only had one class together—American History, a required transfer studies elective. For most of the quarter, I'd been arriving at the last moment and then slipping out the second our professor adjourned class. The day after Jessa Warlow left my bedroom for the last time was different.

After I snapped my book shut, I tossed a tiny piece of rolled-up paper in Matt's direction. It stuck briefly in his hair, then tumbled to the ground.

Matt didn't notice.

I fired a small pencil eraser right between his shoulder blades.

This time, Matt whipped around.

"Sir Lawson," he said as he slid into the desk next to me. All around us, our classmates were packing up their things and heading for the exit.

I nodded. "Fair Maiden Matt."

"To what do I owe this pleasure?"

"There's something I'd like to discuss with you."

Matt glanced around the nearly-empty classroom. "Here?"

"Nah. Let's walk and talk."

Just like we used to do nearly every afternoon, Matt and I got up and headed out of the classroom, through the wide double doors at the front of Gunther Community College, and out onto the lawn.

It was one of those weird March days that looks and feels like winter and spring at the same time. The sun burned bright in a paper-white sky, but blackened slush still lined the curbs and stood in a pile against the community college dumpsters.

Matt and I both reached for our sunglasses. For me, a pair of old aviators my dad had left in the basement. For Matt, some sporty wraparounds.

"So," I said as we started down the sidewalk in the direction of the Gunther Bowl, our default destination, "I know you've got things planned and figured out. You're, you know, college-bound . . ."

Matt eyed me suspiciously. "*But?*"

"But I have a proposal. For your consideration."

"Go on."

"Thom had this idea. That I could move to L.A. and try to get a job in the music industry. Something behind the scenes. At first, I thought the idea was nuts. Now I'm thinking it might not be so crazy after all. Anyway, what I want to know is, if I did go, would you come with me?"

Matt stopped in his tracks. "You want to move to Los Angeles? Last time I talked to you, you wouldn't even move to Philadelphia."

"Things have changed."

"Apparently."

"It's just . . . we've always talked about moving into an apartment. Living in the city—*a* city. So, you know . . . I had to ask."

Matt suddenly looked a little wild. "Really? You had to ask? You don't talk to me for months, and now you want me to give up my scholarship? My summer lab position?"

"You know what? You're right. My question was out of line."

"Out of line? I'm not sure that even begins to cover it."

"I screwed up," I said. "I know that."

"Do you?"

"Yes. Really. I get it."

"And you know I'm fucking with you, right?" Matt's lips curled upward.

"What?"

"I'm messing around!" Matt shoved me, sending me backward so my sneakers sunk into the snow. "My best friend since grade three asks me to move to *L.A.*, and you think I'd say no? If you didn't have the decency to ask me, I'd come along anyway as a stowaway."

I hurried back onto the sidewalk. "Hey, it's just an idea at this point. Something to discuss. I don't have a job lined up or anything." Though Thom had once offered his assistance in that arena, it was pretty obvious his offer was off the table. "I don't even have a car. I'd never take the Nissan—not when Alli's learning to drive."

"What is there to discuss? We'll take my car, of course." Matt drove his late grandfather's Grand Marquis. It was a certified old man car, but spacious—and even a little bit plush. "And I'll apply to the labs at all the universities. With all the schools out there, I'm sure I'll get something."

Matt and I were on the move again. The Gunther Bowl, which was situated on the corner of College Drive and Main, was already in view.

"So when do we go? Summertime?"

Matt shook his head. "No way. The quarter's over at the end of the week. I say we leave after finals."

"What's the rush?" I couldn't wait to put Gunther in the rearview. I wasn't sure how long I could stand living in the same house as my brother. Or the same town as Jessa Warlow. But, as far as I knew, Matt had no reason to flee the town where we'd grown up.

He shrugged. "I don't want to give you time to change your mind."

"Why would I change my mind? This was my idea."

"Sure, but none of this sounds anything like you, Lawson. In fact, I can't help but wonder where these bold new plans of yours are coming from. Should I assume it's your brother's influence?"

"Assume away." Matt could think what he wanted to about my motivations. I didn't want to get into what had gone on between me and Jessa Warlow. Not the musical part, and certainly not the rest. I figured I would save those stories for when Matt and I were old and gray. Or at least twenty-five.

"What are your parents going to say?" I asked as we cut across the Gunther Bowl's parking lot.

"Oh, they won't be pleased," Matt said cheerfully, "but they're used to this sort of thing. Anyway, I'm sure I can make the case for a transfer to USC or UCLA."

I realized that Matt and I were both talking like everything was already decided. Which I guess it was. That meant that in less than a week, I would be *gone.*

I still wasn't sure that California was the place for me, but I suddenly felt like a cinder block had been lifted off my chest.

"This calls for a celebration," Matt said, "drinks on me."

We passed by the familiar collection of rust-scabbed jalopies that were always parked outside of the bowling alley, then threw open the front door and made a beeline for the bar.

It was time to toast what had just become our plans.

~ ~ ~

When I got home from work on Friday night, Allison was waiting up. She took my wrist. "I want to watch old movies," she said. "The ones from when we were kids."

"I can't believe you're leaving in the morning," she said when we sunk into the couch, overstuffed and stained orange in places by the cheese curls of yesteryear. "I want you to go. But I also can't stand it."

I understood completely. On my last night in Gunther, I had what could only be described as mixed feelings. I worried about what would happen in our home when I was gone. I also worried about what might happen to me and Matt, out there in a strange city.

Matt had sent out resumes to all the labs he could think of in the greater L.A. area. He was confident he'd get a bite, but that hadn't happened yet. We were headed for Los Angeles with no jobs and no place to stay. It was something I would never have done before Jessa made a fool out of me.

I tried not to think about any of that. I kept my eyes glued to the cartoon in front of me until I heard Allison snoring. She was fast asleep.

I covered her up with one of my mother's Navajo blankets and headed downstairs to finish packing my things.

While I was still sorting my clothes and cassettes on the area rug beside my bed, my mother appeared. She sat down next to me, long skirt tucked under her, and surveyed my belongings. "You'll need some luggage. Two suitcases at least."

I shrugged. "A couple of garbage will bags will work just as well."

My mother shook her head. "Wait here."

I watched her head for the back of the basement and rummage in the crawl space. Eventually, she located two worn suitcases that I hadn't seen for years. One was covered in tweed, the other peeling white vinyl. They'd both been my mother's when she was a girl.

Slowly, we packed each of them full of my worldly possessions.

When we were finished, I felt very strange. Those two suitcases, lying side by side, reinforced my insignificance in the universe. They also made the fact that I was leaving the town where I grew up really real to me for the first time.

Whether it was really real to my mother, I couldn't say. Earlier that week, when I told her I was going to L.A., she clapped her hands excitedly. "Some of my best days were spent traveling," she gushed. "Me and all my friends used to get in our cars and just *go* when we felt like it. I think this will be good for you, Lawson. You've always been so serious. I mean, sometimes it's like pulling teeth trying to get you to have any fun!"

If she was worried about how she'd handle all the bills after I was gone, she never mentioned it. Instead, my mother gave her old suitcases a pat and left my basement bedroom just as quickly as she'd come.

Chapter 10

On the morning of my departure, I woke up to a bustling house. Everyone was in motion. Thom, who had finally decided to acknowledge my existence, paced from room to room with a cigarette to his lips. My mother sang every song she could think of that glorified life on the road—and, boy, were there a lot of them. Allison, already full-on crying, shoved some scrambled eggs and burnt toast in front of me at the counter.

The whole scene bordered on surreal, but the weirdest part was when Jessa showed up. With no fanfare. She just strolled into our house like she belonged there, appearing well-rested and freshly-scrubbed.

"You need help with anything?" she asked, like she was some kind of old family friend.

I was so surprised that I forgot to maintain a stony silence. "No, I'm all packed and ready to go," I mumbled.

Thom looked away.

A few minutes later, Matt rolled up in the Grand Marquis. While he revved the engine and whooped, I slid on my dad's old aviator sunglasses and picked up my bags. Feeling oddly emotionless, I headed outside with my family and Jessa Warlow in tow. My mother held onto Allison, who was weeping miserably. Thom busied himself lighting a new cigarette.

That left Jessa to help me with my bags. Not that I needed her to or wanted her to. But when I picked up my guitar and my tweed suitcase she grabbed for the other, and there we were, hefting my things into the trunk.

"I can't believe you didn't tell me you were leaving," she hissed through her teeth. "Thom spilled the beans last night."

"I'm sure he's really pleased you're here to see me off."

"I don't care what anybody thinks about it, Lawson. I came here to ask you to stay."

"Why?"

"Because I don't want to lose you." Jessa shifted a few bags around in the trunk, I guess to buy more time. "I know I screwed up. I wasn't thinking about you, or your feelings. Stay here and we'll be together. For real. Like you wanted."

At one time, Jessa's words would have been exactly the ones I wanted to hear. Not anymore. I wanted to be with someone who wanted to be with me, no questions. Not somebody only willing to call me her boyfriend after she was backed against the wall.

I stared into the trunk, at Matt's plain black carry-on and the backpack he used at school. I had an answer for Jessa. Or maybe it was really a test. "I'm not going to stay in Gunther. If you really care about me, drop everything and come out to L.A."

She stepped back. "You mean right now?"

"Not now, but soon. Pack your things and meet me in a couple of weeks."

"That's a lot to ask, Law."

It was, in a way. In another, it wasn't. Jessa had nothing going on in Gunther. She didn't have a job. Now she didn't even have a bandmate. All she had was the temptation to regress with her high school friends, who still thought of her as royalty.

When I looked to Jessa for her reply, she took a deep breath. "We'll see, Law. Give me some time. I'll send out a few resumes and see what I can arrange and, you know, eventually . . ."

Jessa kept speaking, but I stopped listening. I knew we were done. Really, really done. There was nothing substantial in her voice, which got thinner and ultimately less convincing the more she went on.

With a shake of my head, I gave my bags one last shove into place. Then I shut Matt's trunk with a satisfying slam. I wasn't going to sit around Los Angeles waiting for Jessa Warlow to come through on any number of noncommittal half-promises. Just like there was nothing in Gunther for Jessa, there was nothing there for me. It was time to go.

As soon as I stepped away from the car, my family descended. I hugged my mother goodbye, kissed Allison on the face, and shook Thom's outstretched hand. "Good luck," he said sullenly. "Good luck, okay?"

Then Matt let out an ear-splitting yell and took his foot off the break so I had to run, swing the door open, and leap into the passenger seat of Matt's Grand Marquis. Even after I closed the door, I could still hear Allison's wails.

"Hey," Matt said as he cruised down Broad Street. "What's Jessa Warlow doing at your place? Did the queen and king of Gunther finally pair up?"

I leaned back and adjusted my sunglasses. "Who knows why Jessa's there," I said. I couldn't work out Jessa's motivations, and I didn't plan to spend time trying. There was nothing she could say that could make me stay, or even turn around.

If Matt and I were headed for a war-torn country flying the wrong flag, I still would have kept looking straight ahead.

~ ~ ~

The first twenty-four hours on the road, Matt and I were a party on wheels. We drove with the windows down and the radio cranked up. Our energy level was high, our mood decidedly optimistic.

Although we didn't have anything you could call a concrete plan, Matt had already done a phone interview with one lab and received a very promising email from another. He had also assured me that if he got hired, there was a good chance we'd have a shot at cheap dormitory housing.

On day one, the disappointment was the scenery. As it turns out, America isn't a string of national monuments and purple mountain majesties. It's flat, endless farm fields stretching from horizon to horizon.

"Hey buddy . . ." Matt spoke up, somewhere in the middle of corn country. Maybe just to kill time. Or maybe because I hadn't been entirely forthcoming before our departure. "When are you going to tell me why we're really going to L.A?"

"Just like I told you. The music industry's out there. I want to take my shot at a job."

Matt popped open one of the oversized energy drinks he'd packed for our journey. "I mean, why now? And if your brother convinced you to go west, why didn't you just wait to go back with him?"

I didn't exactly want to talk about Jessa Warlow, but Matt had just given up a scholarship to Temple University, probably endured an ear-lashing from his parents, and volunteered to put three-thousand miles on his precious car. I figured I owed him the truth, and probably a lot more.

I shrugged. "Well, Jessa wasn't at my house to see Thom."

"What? Tell me more."

"We've been writing songs together."

"Oh shit. Did Thom set that up?"

"Nope. Jessa came back to Gunther in November. She needed a guitarist. So she called me."

Matt let out a long, low whistle. "Damn! And here I figured you were at old Ralphie's every night, working yourself to death. So, tell me, why aren't you taking your songs to Los Angeles with the illustrious Jessa Warlow at your side?"

"I guess you could say it all went sour."

"How does that happen? How do you *let* that happen?"

"I screwed it up. I got the idea that I was in love with her." The next part was the part I *really* didn't want to talk about. But, like I said, I had decided to give Matt the truth. "There were a lot of late night rehearsals, and we ended up fooling around. Most nights, actually," I explained quickly. "I guess it meant more to me than it did to her."

Matt slapped a hand on the dash. "This was going on since November? And you never said a thing to me? You truly are one of the great enigmas of our time."

"I'm sure you're surprised," I said. "My brother sure was."

"Who says I'm surprised? I never would have guessed it—I mean, how could I?—but it makes sense. You and Jessa Warlow. The only two musicians worth their salt to ever come out of Gunther, Pennsylvania. It's almost too perfect."

"Matt. She dumped me on my ass. For all intents and purposes."

"Of course she did," Matt said cheerfully. "Now you're going out to California to seek your fortune. When you're worthy, she'll come back to you. It'll be beautiful. It'll be magical. It'll be *hot*."

That might have made for a good story in one of the romance novels my mother wrote, but I was living real life. *My life*. I wouldn't make the same mistake twice. Jessa had burned me once. It wouldn't happen again.

~ ~ ~

When the sun came up in the morning, great sheets of rock rose up on either side of the highway. We had cleared the mind-numbing monotony of the bread basket and entered the Rocky Mountains. The sky had also changed, from cloudless blue to gunmetal gray. Dark clouds, swollen with thunderstorms, pressed heavily on the earth.

It was almost unbelievable that we could cross so much of the country so quickly. In sixteen or seventeen more hours, Matt and I would be in Los Angeles, our final destination. I wanted to be filled with nothing but anticipation. Instead, the idea provoked anxiety.

Neither of us had a job, or a lead on a place to stay. We'd put aside some cash—enough for a month of rent at a low- to mid-priced apartment. If we had to come up with a security deposit or last month's rent, we would have to get creative.

A few miles outside of Denver, I eased into a rest area just as the clouds above us shed their moisture. Big globules burst on the windshield, coming faster and faster until the rain was torrential.

"Any word from any of those labs?" I asked as I stared out at the putrid pea soup that served for a view.

"Radio silence."

I nodded. Rain ran in rivers down the windshield. I tried not to think about the fact that we might soon be homeless and jobless in a major city.

Matt, never one to dwell on the possibility of disaster, clapped me on the back. "Hey. Why don't you gas us up? I'm going to get supplies. You know, snacks, some of that canned ravioli, caffeinated beverages. If we're going to drive through the night again—we'll need them."

I did my best to stay positive, but it wasn't easy. Especially when I watched forty of my last travel bucks disappear into the Grand Marquis' thirsty tank.

Chapter 11

After Matt and I crossed into Utah, we didn't see so much as a shanty—or a gas station—for a hundred miles.

The landscape was desolate, and alien to our Pennsylvanian sensibilities. Massive piles of boulders made strange shapes in a desert that looked for all the world like Mars as rendered on a B movie set. I wondered what it would be like to be marooned in the middle of that strange nothingness, with no cell reception and nowhere to crawl to for help.

Just when I was sure that was to be my fate, an old filling station emerged from the mist fifty yards ahead.

"Holy shit," Matt said, "do you see that? I thought we were about to live our own personal horror movie. You know, run out of gas, flag down strange motorists in our desperation, and end up the victims of some hitchhiker-butchering serial killer." He cut the wheel right and pulled up to the nearest pump.

After shelling out Matt's last dollars to the toothless old man who ran the gas station, we were ready to get back on the road.

"Want to switch?" I asked.

"No. I've got this. I'm taking us straight through." Matt grabbed one of the energy drinks we'd stockpiled in Colorado and, eyes locked on the road, blazed us into Nevada.

He was so determined that I really believed we'd make it to Los Angeles, no breaks. But just after dark, Matt veered off the road and brought his car to an abrupt stop that sent both of us bobbing forward.

"I've got to eat," he muttered. Then, before I could give any reply, Matt had already located a four-pack of generic brand pasta and exited the vehicle. He used his keys to break through the cellophane, and then raised a can over his head and tossed it into a nearby boulder.

The aluminum dented, but didn't rupture. Not to be daunted, Matt picked it up and heaved it against a larger, more jagged specimen. This time, the can busted open and ravioli spilled out, in all its glory.

"You see that? Orange gold!" Matt crowed triumphantly.

The sauce *was* an unnatural shade of orange. I figured it must be the preservatives. In that moment, I didn't much care. I got out of the car, selected a can for myself and, after a couple of tosses, my own dinner was prepared. I scooped up the ruptured can and joined Matt on the roomy butt end of the Grand Marquis.

There we sat, at some unknown locale in the Nevada desert, eating ravioli from the can while barbed wire and broken bottles glittered all around us on the roadside. I wouldn't say it was our finest moment, and I wouldn't say I was at my most spirited or optimistic, but the pre-packaged ravioli renewed my strength all the same.

After we feasted, Matt and I leaned our bloated bodies back and stared at the celestial cabaret going on above us. Stars blinked, planets shone, and a few bright objects—definitely either comets or alien spacecraft—jetted across the blackness.

"Why does the sky seem so much bigger here?" Matt asked.

"No idea." Only once I'd left Gunther did I realize how little I actually knew about the world. I had a feeling I still had a lot more to learn. "Think there's any predators roaming around out here? I mean, the man-eating kind."

Matt echoed me. "No idea."

~ ~ ~

Sometime in the middle of the night, I woke up with my teeth chattering.

Matt was already sitting up beside me, hugging himself for warmth. "Goddamn. It has to be thirty degrees!"

"Well, let's get back in the car. I'll drive."

Matt was not amenable. "Fuck that. I have to sleep, Lawson. *Real* sleep."

I knew where he was coming from. I couldn't get any real rest in a moving car either.

So then, we did the only thing we could do. We lugged our suitcases out of the trunk and emptied out all of our clothes into the car.

Matt climbed into a nest of his jeans and T-shirts in the fully-reclined front seat, and I burrowed into the back seat like an animal. Warm in our dens like the rest of the desert fauna, we went to sleep.

~ ~ ~

Early next morning, Matt and I were awakened from precious slumber by the insistent ringing of his cell. While I stretched, Matt roared.

"Idiot! Beast! If this is a telemarketer, I will find out where he lives. I will track him down. And I will destroy him," he threatened. But when Matt finally located his phone and checked the display, his foul mood evaporated.

"Why hello," he said smoothly into the receiver. Then he was mostly just listening, although I heard the occasional "yes," "of course," or "absolutely." Finally, he grabbed some paper out of the glove box and scribbled down an address.

The anticipation was intense. "Explain," I said the second he hung up. "Please."

Matt, clearly sensing my urgency, took a moment to stretch. "Well, as it turns out, the UCal lab decided that I'm an all-around mensch and would no doubt be an asset to their team. Apparently, they tried to call yesterday, but couldn't get through. Probably due to the lack of phone service available in the desert wilderness."

"Jesus." *Sweet relief.* "They offer dormitory housing?"

"Not to non-students."

"So we're on our own."

Matt put up a hand. "Slow down, old buddy. You didn't let me finish. As it turns out, the lab had an assistant who recently went back home to Iowa or Idaho or some other bumblefuck and won't be back until fall at the soonest."

I raised my head. "So, what does that mean for us?"

"It means she would be positively elated if we, or anybody really, finished out her lease as subletters. Provided we don't destroy her furniture and pay the rent in a timely fashion each month."

I sat back against the seat and breathed out a long, slow sigh of relief. Somehow, despite all the odds, our collective ass was not grass. Matt and I would not be sharing a box in some forsaken Los Angeles alley. We'd be living in our own apartment. And we wouldn't even need to go dumpster cruising for furniture.

~ ~ ~

As cerulean morning blanched to burning white afternoon, civilization crept into view. Shopping centers and landscaping and miles of suburbs filled with squat, sand-colored houses reared up against the brilliant sky. Then, before Matt and I were even really ready for it—we saw the first signs for Los Angeles.

I guess you could say we lost it. I can't think of any better way to put it. Matt pushed his chest out and spread his arms like wings, steering with only a knee. I stuck one leg out the window and swung halfway out of the car, pumping my right fist in the air. We veered wildly all the while.

When I ducked back inside, Matt delivered a series of punches to my shoulder. "We're here, man. We're in Elllll Lay. Can you believe this shit?"

"Lay off." I rubbed my arm, but I was laughing. "You're crazy."

When the downtown skyline finally broke through the clouds (or maybe it was smog), we headed straight for it. I watched in silence as the buildings grew larger in the cloudless sky.

As we entered the city, the freeway rose up, and I peered down at the sea of neighborhoods below. The gray pallor I had come to associate with cityscapes, it seemed, did not apply. Homes and strip malls were covered in pink and orange stucco. Garish signs rose up in front of shrubbery that was positively Pleistocene. It was all so foreign and exotic. Like nothing I had seen before. Like nothing I'd imagined.

Just before we reached downtown L.A.'s towering collection of skyscrapers, Matt broke from the flow of traffic and we exited the freeway.

We passed a few more strip malls, then, all at once, we were surrounded by stately mansions on neatly clipped lawns. At first, I couldn't believe we were in the right place. Then I noticed the cluster of mailboxes next to each front door, and I caught on: The mansions had been broken up into separate apartments. A whole lot of them.

After a few quick turns, Matt came to a stop in front of a wide stucco manor house that stood three stories tall. He turned to me. "Well," he said, "this is it."

And then the car was lurching alternately backward and forward, as Matt completed one of the most inept parallel parking jobs in history. Five or six attempts later, the Grand Marquis was located passably close to the curb, and we climbed out onto the street.

After ringing the manager at the entrance and signing a few pages of paperwork, Matt and I became apartment renters and official citizens of Los Angeles, California. As we unlocked number 2F, I felt a little thrill work its way through my guts. I was acutely aware that my first apartment was behind the thick slab of wood in front of me.

When the door creaked open, I passed right by Matt and stepped inside. I couldn't help myself. My eyes were everywhere, hungry for information. I took in a respectably sized living room with a fresh coat of terra cotta paint, wood floors, and a couple of couches. An open doorway on the left led to a kitchenette; a door on the right to a small but cozy bedroom complete with a double bed.

All I knew was everything was more than I could have asked for, and it was all ours. I wandered into the center of the living room and sat down on the floor. I guess you could say I was overwhelmed.

~ ~ ~

When I woke and stumbled out of the bedroom after my first night as a resident of Los Angeles, California, the living room was all alight. The sun bounced off the hardwood, making the dust swirling in the air sparkle.

I went to the window and took a good look at the world I now inhabited. Tall palm trees swayed against a purplish morning sky and the ancient manor houses in salt water taffy colors stretched to the main road. There, cars vroomed and chugged and exhaled exhaust.

When I pulled my head back inside the apartment, I grabbed Matt's phone, which he'd left charging in the living room, and dialed Alli's cell.

It was almost time for school to start, and I wasn't sure Allison would pick up, but pick up she did. She screamed so loudly into the receiver that I almost dropped Matt's phone.

"You made it! Where are you right now?"

The inconsolable girl I'd left in Gunther was gone. I smiled wide. "We got an apartment. In a neighborhood near downtown Los Angeles."

"An apartment. In *California*," Allison said, seeming to turn the word over on her tongue. "What's it like? Does it feel different there?"

"It does," I said without thinking. "Even the air is different—more restless, I guess—and there's this sweet scent everywhere."

"What are you going to do first?" Allison breathed.

I peered out the window, at the strange new scenery. I was in a new city. I could feel its expanse pulsing around me. The urban wilderness, made up of places I'd heard about in legends and movies and songs, begged to be explored. And yet a more pressing concern ensured that any adventuring would have to wait. Namely, my need for gainful employment.

"I'm going to get a job," I told Alli.

I had no leads, and no connections, but I was hopeful. Mostly because I'd noticed something of great interest on the way from the freeway—a pizza shop with a line out the door.

Chapter 12

After Matt set out in his lab-rat best to go fill out new hire forms at UCal, I set out to find the establishment that had caught my eye. If there was anything I knew, it was how to put together a pizza. And if there was anything I knew about kitchens, it was that the turnover was high. Some guy was always getting tossed out on his ass or just stopped showing up, leaving an opening for the next guy willing to work long hours at a mostly thankless job.

The pizza shop I'd spotted wasn't hard to find. Although it was located on a nondescript stretch of a nearby avenue and marked only with a dusty sign that spelled out "Pizza Kitchen," the place appeared to be having some kind of moment. The line was not only long—it was also populated mainly by the tragically hip. I watched them pose and scroll through their phones in their bored, tragically hip way.

With nothing to lose, I stepped inside and marched up to a register manned by a jowly man with one thick, angry eyebrow. He was at that very moment doling out change to a few of his customers. "You hiring in the back?" I asked loudly enough to be heard over the tinkle of glassware and the constant chatter in the packed dining room.

"I'm busy," the man snapped. "Talk to John." He glanced over his shoulder in the general direction of the kitchen.

"Yes, sir." I did as I was told and moved stiffly behind the cash register and into the kitchen, where I was hit by a wall of sweltering heat and the stink of sweat and pepperoni. A few guys were rolling out dough and doling out toppings with impressive speed. A few more were loading the ovens with pizza paddles.

"Is there a John here?" I asked, bracing myself for a brush-off.

After a few beats, one of the guys—presumably John—took off his gloves, wiped some sweat from his brow, and made his way through the tables to shake my hand.

He wore an apron over his T-shirt and a hairnet over a well-oiled slickback. His teeth were worse than mine. A lot worse. "So you want to work," he said, none too kindly.

"That's what I'm here for."

"Can you work *hard?*" Little drops of spit landed on my shirt. "I'm sick of fucking Hep Cat Joe strolling in here asking for a job because it's where his friends hang out on Friday nights, and then walking out on the first shift because his shoulders are sore and the exhaust fan is fucked."

"I won't do that," I promised. "I need the work. I'll stick around, and I'll take any overtime you've got."

John squinted, as if trying to decide whether he believed me. Finally, he grabbed an apron and a snood from a nearby bin and shoved them in my direction.

"You can start now. The guy out front—George—owns the place. He'll pay you in cash till we get your paperwork squared away."

~ ~ ~

I took my first and only break of the day with John, who relaxed once he realized I wasn't going to turn in my apron on day one. We stood out in the back parking lot against one of the chain-link fences while John sucked down a cigarette.

"Why'd you move to L.A. anyway?" he asked. "I grew up here, so it always perplexes me. Why people keep coming in droves, to this dismal, overcrowded place."

"I want to work in the music industry," I explained, just like I had to Matt. "My brother said there's jobs to be had, but he decided I was public enemy number one before I could make use of any of his connections or anything."

John snickered. "That's sibling rivalry for you. You know, I used to play upright bass in a few different psychobilly bands. Got a lot of gigs. Had to give it up, though."

"Why?"

"Got a kid now. I need a steady paycheck. I don't know anybody who could give you a job, but I can hook you up with somebody who'd take you to see some bands. Can't promise any more than that."

"I'm willing to start anywhere," I said.

"All right. Well, I'm not in touch with most of the cats I used to hang around with, but there is someone who comes to mind. She's the cousin of one of my old buddies. A real fangirl. Comes in here on a semi-regular basis."

"Can you get me in touch?"

"Sure. Next time I see her, I'll send her your way." John flicked his cancer stick. "Now, let's get back in there. George doesn't like it when I leave the chuckleheads on the line to their own devices."

~ ~ ~

When I returned to the apartment after my first shift, Matt stared at me, perplexed. "What the hell is that thing on your head?"

I snatched off my snood and stuffed it in my pocket.

"And what is that smell? It's like . . . salted meat product created in an onion factory."

"I'm making pizza again. The state of the kitchen makes Ralphie's a modern, top-of-the-line establishment in comparison, but the owner promised overtime."

Matt wrinkled his nose. "Sure you don't want to hold out for something more civilized?"

"Nope." I most certainly did not. My pockets were full, and Pizza Kitchen was just a few blocks away. Perhaps even more importantly, John was going to help me get in touch with his friend. A certain Teresa Ramos who knew L.A.'s underground music scene "inside-out."

~ ~ ~

As it turned out, my job at Pizza Kitchen was perfect for me at that time in my life. The heat was nearly unbearable, the breaks were few and far between, and the exhaust fan was indeed fucked. But it also felt good to work that hard and that long. Even purifying.

All the bitterness and hurt I'd felt those last days in Gunther leaked out of my pores, exiting my body with the toxins. Still, I hadn't come all the way to California to make pizza, the same thing I'd been doing since I was fifteen years old. I wanted to find my way into L.A.'s music scene, and I was counting on John's connection. He promised she'd stop by soon, and all I could do was wait.

Unfortunately, as the week wore on, there was no sign of his "too cool for school" customer. All I could figure out was that this Teresa girl had better things to do than cart my ass around town. Or else she'd simply pegged me as a lame transplant—or a charity case. But then, just when I considered myself officially blown off . . . there was a shoe.

I was standing out behind Pizza Kitchen in my snood, half blinded by the setting sun, when a worn Chuck Taylor came skidding by. It flipped over once, then came to rest, right side up near the dumpsters. I stared at it in blank wonderment.

When I finally lifted my gaze, I saw the lean figure of a girl waving from behind the parking lot's chain-link fence. She stood next to a mud-brown beater of a car.

"Hey!" she called out. "You Lawson?"

"Uh, yes," I called back. "And you're Teresa? Teresa Ramos?"

She nodded. "That I am. And I've been trying to get your attention for a full five minutes. Hence the projectile."

With that, Teresa approached the fence, surveyed it, then climbed right over with surprising ease.

"Haven't done that for a while," she said, pushing her cropped hair out of her face.

I looked her over. Teresa was very slight and decked out in a colorless ensemble of ripped gray jeans and a faded band T-shirt. Big tea-colored eyes peered up at me from under a row of jet black bangs.

"John told me to come back here." Teresa tipped her chin in my direction. "But he didn't tell me you were *hot*." She clapped a hand over her mouth. "Did I really just say that out loud?"

I wasn't sure how to answer. So I didn't.

Teresa colored, giggled, and raced off to retrieve her shoe. When she returned, she had recovered. "Anyway," she said, "John tells me you want to see a rock show."

The phrase "rock show" rang strange in my ears. It sounded like something a teenager would say. In fact, everything about John's friend-of-a-friend seemed juvenile. Her enthusiasm, her mannerisms. Her unfiltered speech.

"Hey," I said suddenly, "You know what? I really appreciate you coming back here, but I think we should call this off."

Teresa frowned. "Why?"

"It's just—you seem to be a little younger than the people I usually hang around with."

"Okay. Well, I'm twenty. How old are *you?*"

I hesitated. I hadn't expected her to bounce my question back to me, and I knew my answer wouldn't go over well. "Twenty-one," I admitted.

Teresa's hands moved to her hips. "Oh, I'm so impressed. A whole year older and wiser."

"Let me explain . . ."

She made a sound of disgust. "I don't know how they do things wherever you're from, but in L.A. we grow up fast."

"I'm from P.A."

She spit on the ground. "*Pennsylvania*. While you and your buddies were tipping cows and dreaming about places like L.A., me and my friends were living in a big city, with culture, and millions of people, and the entire goddamn entertainment industry. I don't know where you get off . . . "

"Where is this club anyway?" I interrupted. "The one you wanted to go to?"

"What do you care?" she snarled.

"Because I want to go."

Teresa blinked. "Wait. I mean . . . you do?"

"Yes. If you still want me to." The thing was, even if this girl Teresa wasn't the girl I was expecting, or maybe even hoping for—she had moxie. I had been dismissive, but she'd stood her ground and given me a much-deserved piece of her mind.

"Well," Teresa stuttered. "Sure I do. I mean, of course I do."

Before I could change my mind, she produced a magic marker from her pocket, grabbed my hand, and wrote the venue address directly on my arm.

"See you Friday," she said, "*downtown*."

Chapter 13

After work on Friday night, I showered up and caught the train. I wasn't intimately familiar with downtown Los Angeles, but most of the streets were laid out in a loose grid. I figured I'd get off at Union Station, then follow the numbered streets to the address Teresa had marked on my skin.

I expected to find a little Friday commotion, but after a quick eastward ride, I stepped out into an empty world. Theaters with crumbling marquees and once-grand hotels rose up in the city silence, their windows covered by cardboard and signs advertising cheap weekly rates. Apparently, downtown's flophouse inhabitants had retreated into their dens to administer their drugs or contend with their illnesses. They knew enough not to venture out onto the streets at night, when they might get hassled or stabbed. I, of course, did not have the same foresight.

Just when I was sure I was in the wrong neighborhood, I turned the corner and the scene changed entirely. The constant chatter of concertgoers ricocheted off the brick and concrete faces of the warehouses that lined the street, sending ghostly echoes into the night. Bodies stood here and there in front of a warehouse in the center of the block, and a great many more swarmed its entrance like so many bees.

Relieved, I stuck my hands in my pockets and hurried down the sidewalk toward the hive. I was just beginning to wonder how I was going to find Teresa in all the madness when a strange, unpleasant sensation shot through my insides and sent me leaping clear off the pavement. *Had I been shot?*

Stabbed? Stung? No. Somebody had jammed a finger into the sensitive skin between my rib cage and my pelvic bone.

When I whipped around, I found Teresa looking much the same as she did when I'd met her—jeans, T-shirt, jet black hair cut bluntly at her chin.

She giggled. "You made it."

I shook my head and rubbed my side. "Why didn't you tell me what kind of neighborhood this place was in? I would have borrowed my roommate's car and picked you up."

"Unnecessary." Teresa's eyes drifted upward. "I live here. They gutted this warehouse a long time ago and put in efficiency apartments. It's supposed to be one to a room, but my best friend's letting me crash until I can get a place in Hollywood."

Right on cue, a diminutive young man in thick-rimmed glasses sauntered up. "Lucky you, to have a date Friday night!"

Teresa narrowed her eyes. "I told you this isn't a date, Dylan."

"You don't have to be a bitch," he complained.

"I'll show you 'bitch.'" Teresa grabbed hold of Dylan's arms, wrapped them behind his back, and wrestled a pack of cigarettes out of his pocket.

When Teresa stepped back and lit up, Dylan straightened himself out and sniffed. "Light me too?"

"Of course." Graciously, Teresa extended her lighter. Dylan bent down and sucked, his hands cupping the flame against the breeze.

"You said he's your best friend?" I asked when Dylan wandered off, smoking sullenly.

"He's not always like that. He got stood up tonight."

"Oh. Ouch."

"Yeah. He's hung up on this guy Parker. But Dylan has to realize that one blowie on a fire escape doesn't mean you have Friday plans for the rest of the year."

I cleared my throat. I still wasn't used to the way Teresa talked. You know . . . no filter.

"Anyway." She tossed her cigarette on the ground and crushed it under her sneaker. "We should go in. We'll want to get a good spot."

At the gaping maw of the club, a few wide steps led to a huge, grimy basement. The dank space had the appearance of a torture chamber, but someone had taken great pains to convert it into a respectable venue. Across the expanse of stained concrete, a high wooden stage was surrounded by lights and an impressive array of speakers. There was no bar, but at our feet dozens of beer cans floated in a kiddie pool.

I bent down and fished out two. Then I inspected a metal container on the wall with a slot for bills—the kind they had at my own apartment building for depositing rent checks when the manager wasn't in. "Honor system?"

Teresa nodded. "For those who can afford it. Unlimited access to cheap American beer is supposed to keep all the runaways that live here off the pipe. You know—the lesser of two evils."

"Ah. I see." This strange downtown world was clearly old hat to Teresa. To me, it was all new, and rather peculiar.

After I stuffed a few bills into the pay slot, Teresa took hold of my arm and we wound our way toward the back of the room. From our position near the stage, we watched some teenaged musicians in coordinated black and red clothing set up their gear and check their sound with the help of a ginger-headed engineer.

"This band won't be good," Teresa informed me as the crowd filled in behind us.

"How do you know?"

"I know those kids. They live here. But the headliner is always great. The wait will be worth it."

Moments later, the so-called rock show began. The singer—a guy wearing a lot of makeup—screamed continuously while the band struggled to play four chords in time. A willowy keyboardist noodled away for nearly the whole set but not in any way that matched what the rest of the band was doing. Still, the crowd cheered. I didn't have to ask why. These were their friends. The cool kids.

When I looked at Teresa for her assessment, she rolled her eyes. I couldn't help liking that she was unimpressed. I stood a little closer to her.

Finally, the band played one last, overwrought note. The multitudes around us clapped and whooped. Teresa tugged on my sleeve.

"We should stay up front and save our spots," she said, up on tiptoes so she could speak into my ear. "Like I said, this next band will be great."

"After that last performance, I don't know if I believe you."

"Really. Then let's make a wager." Teresa grinned.

For the first time, I really noticed her smile. Her teeth were very white and small, and all situated in a neat row. "What are the terms?"

"If this band is good—like really, really good—you've got to give me a kiss."

I raised an eyebrow. Teresa was younger and more waifish than the girls I noticed on the street. Girls like, well . . . Jessa. Teresa was also more talkative and eager than the people I was used to. But those differences were refreshing. Also, I won't lie—it flattered me that a kiss would be like a prize to her. Or at least some kind of thrill.

"You're on."

She flushed as the headlining band moved into place. After the drummer slammed the snare four times, the band plowed into the first song and, all at once, the whole room was bouncing. The wiry singer-slash-bassist moved around the stage with liquid fluidity, and all eyes were on him.

However, I was most impressed with the drummer. His bald head grew ever shinier as he delivered massive beats that kept the room throbbing.

Teresa and I stayed near the stage until the very last second of the very last encore. Then Teresa turned to me with shining eyes. She had won, and she knew it. "Let's go sit down!"

I followed her through the crowd until we reached a cluster of plastic lawn furniture kitty-corner to the kiddie pool.

We both took a chair.

"Okay. I'm ready!" Teresa smoothed her poker-straight hair and leaned in.

I laughed and grabbed Teresa's chin.

She put up her hands. "Stop! Don't go so fast. I want to make this last."

Ignoring her protests, I planted a quick kiss on her lips.

Teresa shrunk in disappointment, but before she could call "no fair," I pulled her in again and gave her a real kiss.

When our tongues flicked together briefly, I felt her shiver. She stared at her lap. "That was fucking amazing."

"Care to place any more wagers?"

She put a hand to her head. "I think I need some air."

"Let's get some."

I grabbed for Teresa's hand and, suddenly, we were moving through the crowd, toward the open doors. The second we cleared them, Teresa launched herself into my arms with a gazelle-like leap.

Mid-makeout, Dylan approached, wearing a sour expression. When he thumped an index finger on Teresa's shoulder, she whirled around, eyes blazing. "*What?*"

"Tim's about to start his set. I thought you might like to know."

"Oh!" The fire left Teresa's eyes. "He's early."

She slid back onto the concrete. "We've got to see Tim spin," she said, as if I should know who "Tim" was. "Come on!"

Inside the cavernous space, the floor shook with booming electronic music. Just to the side of the stage, the sound engineer, now wearing dark sunglasses and ensconced in the DJ booth, bobbed his ginger head.

"I never used to care about electronic music before," Teresa yelled over the thumping music. "I didn't understand why anybody would want to listen to music somebody made on a computer—or without a guitar. Then Tim started spinning here every week. He knows electronic stuff like nobody else. I think," she said, "he might be a genius."

Most of the kids around us were dancing energetically, but Teresa didn't move a muscle. Instead, she stood with her arms folded, listening intensely. I did the same, taking in music that was unlike anything I'd heard in my father's cassette collection. A slamming four-on-the-floor beat was the only constant. Seething synthesizers and otherworldly blips created a landscape of sound I could almost see in front of my eyes.

I couldn't believe how quickly two hours passed—I guess you could say I was hypnotized. Around three a.m. the lights came up. The party was over. But while the rest of the crowd stretched and meandered slowly toward the back doors, Teresa shot forward, toward the DJ booth.

I hustled to catch up, and then there we were, in Tim the DJ's personal space. Up close, he was just a regular guy of about thirty in rumpled jeans and Converse.

He took off his sunglasses, revealing a set of pale blue eyes crinkled at the edges with early laugh lines.

"You ready?" Teresa asked. She trembled with excitement.

Tim stopped packing up his gear. "Go on."

Teresa spit out a bunch of strange, exotic-sounding words in rapid succession. I couldn't image what kind of code she was speaking in. Then, finally, I caught on. She was naming the artists Tim had played.

When Teresa finished, Tim held out his hand to shake. "You did your homework," he said. Then he turned to me. "Teresa knows just about every rock band out there, even if they only played one note, in the middle of the night. I told her if she studied up on her electronic music, I'd let her check out my music collection. I've got a little bit of everything." He shrugged. "Okay, a lot of everything."

Teresa clapped her hands. "Can we go now?"

Tim frowned. "*We?* I said you could come."

"I wasn't trying to invite myself," I said quickly. "I didn't know anything about this."

"I'm only giving Teresa a hard time. Come along . . ."

"Lawson," Teresa supplied.

"Yes," he said, "come along, Lawson, and we'll all head to Hollywood. I'm assuming you two probably had a beer or two, so you can catch a ride with me. As long as you don't mind taking the train back here."

"We don't mind," Teresa assured him.

As Tim packed up the last of his gear into a heavy canvas bag, I studied his small, sturdy laptop, portable turntable, and numerous cables, each of which he wound and fastened with Velcro.

"How do you control everything with that laptop?" I blurted out.

"It's all the magic of software, my friend."

"Oh." I could tell Tim expected a knowing chuckle, but I didn't really get him.

I guess that was obvious. "Don't worry," he told me, "I'll show you all my gear when we get to Hollywood. There will be plenty of time. I'm sure Teresa's going to be eyeballs deep in vinyl for most of the night."

With that, Tim slung his bag onto his back, and the three of us headed across the concrete floor, out onto the street, and into the parking garage next door.

While I climbed into the back of Tim's Honda Civic, it hit me that I was going to see Hollywood for the first time. I'd always assumed Hollywood must be a pretty glamorous spot, but I'd heard John dismiss it repeatedly as a "shithole"—an assessment that, somehow, only deepened its mystery.

Chapter 14

Tim's little Honda purred through the eldritch streets of downtown Los Angeles. After a few blocks the old hotels and converted theaters gave way to spanking new granite bank buildings, behemoth fountains, and those huge, twisted pieces of iron they call commercial art. A few minutes later, we were winding through the green lawns of Los Feliz. Then we were on Hollywood Boulevard.

I pressed my face up against the window glass and took in a shadowy district lit by aging neon. Short, twisted trees lined streets decorated with cracked pink stars. For every head shop and porn emporium, there were three souvenir stores featuring tiny plastic Oscars and cheap T-shirts splashed with the faces of old movie stars.

To me, Hollywood seemed like a place that was doing its best to live with the ghost of itself. There was something noble in the struggle, something elegant in the decay. That made me like Hollywood better than I expected to.

At the famous crux of Hollywood and Highland, Tim hung a right, then slowed in front of a brick apartment building guarded by an arched wrought-iron gate at least eight feet tall. Pillars flanked a fire escape that snaked up to the fifth floor.

Tim turned to face me and Teresa. "This is it, folks."

~ ~ ~

A quick glance around Tim's living room left me in awe. It was half the size of my living room in Koreatown and jam-packed with electronics, musical instruments, and boxes stuffed with records. The nerve center was a desk topped with a pair of speakers and a wide monitor.

As soon as Tim set down his canvas duffel, he sat in front of that desk, fired up the computer, and sent music with pounding bass surging through the speakers.

Teresa settled onto the couch. It was a hunched, torn affair in faded blue, but I knew the guitars above it had to cost thousands of dollars each. There was an old Les Paul the color of tooth enamel, a gleaming new Stratocaster, and two acoustics, both polished to a high shine.

While Teresa lugged a box of records onto her lap, I leaned over Tim's desk. "You need all this stuff to put together your DJ sets?"

"Not exactly. DJing is really a side gig for me. I'm an audio engineer. That's how I get the cash to buy—you guessed it—more audio equipment."

Before Tim could explain any more, there was a rap at the door. He immediately hopped to his feet. After a glance through the peephole, Tim unfastened the stout metal latch and let in a woman sporting a big, eye-scrunching smile. Her eyes swept the room. "Ah. Guests!"

"This is Lydia," Tim introduced. "My significantly better half. And *this* is Teresa, my self-professed biggest fan—and her friend Lawson."

Lydia shook out her tightly-coiled curls and kicked off her loafers. "Well, it's a pleasure. Hope you don't mind if I unwind. I just did nine hours of hard time at the Franklin Hotel."

"She's their concierge extraordinaire," Tim clarified when Lydia didn't.

Lydia gave a little bow, curled up on the end of the couch opposite Teresa, and produced a tiny metal pipe from inside her dress. While she packed it with what I could only assume was marijuana, an orange cat emerged from under the couch and stretched out, purring, in her lap. "I call him

The Prince," she said, as bluish smoke poured from between her lips.

"The cat?" I asked automatically.

"Oh, no. That's Gargamel." Lydia giggled. "I was talking about my bowl. Here," she said, "meet him."

When I declined, Lydia handed her pipe to Teresa, who did the old spark-up-and-inhale with a casual kind of ease. Through the haze of her exhaled smoke, I noticed Tim beckoning from his position behind the desk.

"Me?" I asked dumbly.

"Yeah. You. *Lawson*." He pointed to a small recliner in the corner. "Pull up a chair."

"Oh. Okay." I dragged the recliner toward Tim's desk. "I don't even know what half of this stuff is," I admitted.

"Well, I'll explain. Even better—I'll show you." Tim manipulated the mouse and opened a program. When he selected a file, a bunch of horizontal rows appeared on the screen. "I mix all of my clients' tracks right here. I get the levels right, and the EQ. I apply effects.

"Okay." I gestured to the rack next to me, full of blinking electronics. "What are all these?"

"Well, these right here are compressors. Then we've got the power conditioner, a sound module, a pre-amp, a sonic maximizer. And effects . . . if you want effects . . . well, I've got *effects*."

"You record in here too?"

"Sure. Everything except drums. I rent time at one of the pro studios for those. Although quite a few of the bands I work with use programmed beats. That's one of my specialties."

"Your neighbors don't mind?" Tim's apartment was on the corner next to the stairs, so he wouldn't share a wall with any of his neighbors. But I was pretty sure there was a unit directly below.

Tim stomped on the floor. "Nobody's down there. Thanks to a fortuitous black mold issue."

"Fortuitous black mold issue," Lydia repeated from the couch. She dissolved into giggles.

Tim swiveled around to shoot Lydia a grin. Then he turned back to me. "You play any instruments?"

"Guitar. A little bass."

"Good. I can show you exactly what I do." Tim spun around in his chair, crossed the room in two steps, and reached over Lydia's head to take down his Les Paul. He handed it my way.

While I cradled the guitar in my lap, Tim connected a cable from the guitar to a box in one of the racks next to his desk. "Play," he instructed.

I did. Little crumpled lines moved across the screen. "Fuck." It was all I could think of to say. I'd never recorded a single note before, and there it was—my riff captured forever. My mind, I guess you could say, was blown.

~ ~ ~

In the morning, I woke up all at once when a beam of sunlight shot into the back of my eye socket like a laser. At first, I had no idea where I was, or how I'd come to be there. Then I glanced right and saw Tim next to me, still working busily on the recording we'd made of our wee-hours jam session.

When I nudged him, he removed his headphones.

"Sorry, man. Didn't mean to make a night of it."

"No sweat. I think we came up with some good stuff. We can polish it up next time you come over."

Next time. So Teresa and I hadn't worn out our welcome. I turned around to see if she'd heard, but she was still asleep, her form wedged between Lydia and Gargamel.

When I crept toward Teresa and touched her shoulder, she stirred. Her tea-colored eyes flicked open. "We really stayed all night?" She squinted her eyes against the sun, which flooded the room and painted bright grids in the shape of the window on the carpet and the walls. "What time is it?"

"Ten thirty."

"Oh, no!" she whispered loudly. "Dylan just got me a job at a vintage shop on Hollywood Boulevard. I can't be late." Teresa quickly but carefully extricated herself from the sofa without waking Lydia or her sleeping feline.

After thanking Tim for letting us stay, Teresa and I hastened down the stairs, out onto Highland, then south to Hollywood Boulevard. The whole time, Teresa was humming. A few times I saw her skip.

"You know what?" she said as we waited to cross at the light, surrounded by swarms of tourists. "I think last night was the best night of my life!"

Her claim was, I assumed, hyperbole. At the same time, I couldn't help but think that something magical had happened in Tim and Lydia's apartment. I should by every right have been dead tired. Instead, I trembled with some new energy. I wasn't sure, but it felt a little like inspiration.

~ ~ ~

Back at home, Matt was up and at 'em. While I unlocked the apartment door, I could hear him singing something in the style of Luciano Pavarotti. As I stepped into the living room, Matt peered around the corner, revealing a face well-coated in shaving cream.

"All-nighter, eh?" he asked with a sly grin. "Think I wouldn't find out?"

I couldn't even answer. I just stood in the middle of the living room like an idiot.

Matt's eyes widened. "Hey, what's wrong with you, kid? That must have been some chick!"

He disappeared, and I heard the sound of running water. When he came out to inspect me, his face was clean. "I stayed out all night with John's friend Teresa," I explained, "but we didn't go back to her place. We went to her friend's apartment, and he had all of this recording equipment rigged up right there in the living room. He let me try out his gear and mess with his computer programs and everything. We jammed all night."

Matt nodded. "Intriguing. I'm not surprised you're into that stuff, Law. You have the patience."

And then, accepting that there were no lurid details to coax out of me, Matt returned to the bathroom to finish his morning routine.

"Mind if I use your phone?" I called.

"Go ahead!"

I grabbed Matt's phone from the charging dock, took a seat on the futon, and dialed Allison.

She picked up quickly, the way she always did when she saw Matt's phone number flashing on her phone.

"Alli," I said, without even giving a greeting, "I think I've decided what I want to do. Or what I want to be." I tried to remember what Tim had called himself. His official title. For a few seconds, I blanked. Then it came to me. "An audio engineer."

"Oh," Allison said breezily, "how do you become one of those?"

"I don't know," I admitted.

But I was sure as hell going to find out.

Chapter 15

After a few more nights spent jamming in Tim's apartment, something truly amazing happened. Teresa quietly arranged for me to work as Tim's intern. It was something I probably would not have thought of myself, and certainly wouldn't have been bold enough to ask for. And yet it was one of the best things to happen to me in my twenty-one years on earth.

The first day I reported for duty as an intern felt like a solemn occasion. I stepped into Tim's apartment, the headphones Allison had given me for Christmas hanging around my neck. Finally, I'd be able to use them for something more than listening to my dad's old box sets, and playing along before bed.

"You know I can't pay you, right?" Tim said when I sat down next to him at the spanking new desk chair that had appeared next to his. "Of course, you're free to use the studio to record your own music whenever you want to. That's the only perk I can offer right now."

"Understood." I wasn't looking for perks. I wanted to learn to mix so I could be an audio engineer like Tim. As for my own music—the songs I'd written with Jessa—I hadn't thought about them since I'd left Gunther. A vision of Jessa and I strumming our guitars on mustard shag flickered into my mind. Just as quickly, it evaporated.

I nodded. "I'm ready."

"First things first," Tim said. "We'll start with note-by-note editing. If you're not crazy after a few hours of that, maybe audio engineering really is for you."

While I watched carefully, Tim showed me how to zoom in close and move drum hits and other notes onto the little lines that represented each beat. Then he let me try.

When we listened back, the difference was obvious. Even dramatic. What had once sounded more like a lot of noise and fuzz than a song had become a perfectly respectable punk rock ditty.

Tim grinned at my obvious surprise. "We haven't even applied pitch correction yet."

"Do all of your projects start like this?"

"No. But a lot of them do. Three-quarters of the frustrated actors in Los Angeles have the same idea—to front a band. Half the kids in Beverly Hills have a rich uncle willing to pay for a record they can hand out at school. Everybody's got the big dream disease around here. Doesn't mean they can play for shit. But after I'm done with their tracks, the wannabes sound like a million bucks. That's where the money is right now. At least . . . my money."

"I get it."

"Good." Tim opened a new file. "Let's try another track."

I couldn't wait. There was something satisfying about smoothing, correcting, and perfecting. The hours raced by.

"Damn," Tim said hours later, "It's already seven o'clock."

I sat back in my chair. "You need me to get out of your way?"

"Actually . . . I've got a band coming in to record vocals any minute. I could use an assistant if you don't mind playing gopher."

I didn't. Tim and I were still turning his coat closet into a makeshift vocal booth when a girl in a short yellow dress and a guy in a tight turtleneck showed up.

"This is Brian," Tim introduced, "and this is Joan. Founding members of Hollywood Death Star."

I straightened. I had heard of HDS. Through Teresa. They were local indie darlings, famous for using vintage instruments—analog synthesizers, ancient theremins, junkshop beat machines. Clearly, Tim's roster included more than the amateurs and wannabes who were his bread and butter.

As it turned out, Joan and Brian were also excellent vocalists who sang all their parts in harmony. It was *California Dreamin'*. It was *Pet Sounds*. It was perfection. I stayed until three a.m. fetching, assembling, tightening, and pouring glasses of water.

I had an opening shift at Pizza Kitchen to look forward to the next morning, but I didn't care. I would have stayed all night.

~ ~ ~

Nearly every evening, as soon as I got home from Pizza Kitchen I changed my shirt, hopped onto the train or the gently used bicycle I'd acquired for commuting purposes, and headed for Tim's place. I didn't see much of Matt, but I still made it out to a show or two every week with Teresa. And I never, ever missed a call with Allison.

At least once a week I called her from my newly acquired phone. She kept me informed about the state of affairs at home—chaotic but tolerable—and I told her everything that happened in the studio.

Occasionally, I said a quick hello to my mom. Never to my brother. Until, one day, Allison made a quiet request—one of the very few things she had asked for since I'd left.

"I think," she said, "that you should talk to Thom."

"Oh." I took a deep breath. I hadn't spoken with him since the morning I jumped into Matt's moving Grand Marquis. And why? Because of a lot of drama that already felt like ancient history. It was all kids' stuff, and no reason to cut Thom out of my life.

"Do you think Thom wants to talk to me?" I ventured.

"He would never say so, but . . . I do think that, Law."

I was going to talk to my brother. Because Allison wanted me to. And because it was time. "Will you get him for me?" I asked.

"Of course I will!" Alli exclaimed. I could hear the smile in her voice. "Hold on."

Fifteen or twenty seconds later, the line crackled. "Law? Hey."

"Hey." I cleared my throat. "Hey, Thom. How are you?"

"Great," he said a little too smoothly. "Couldn't be better."

"Okay. I mean, glad to hear it."

"Yeah."

The silence on the line wasn't the comfortable kind. I searched for something to say. "I'm surprised you're still in Gunther. I was expecting to hear that you'd cut out for California again any day."

"Nah. I had a lot of fun out in L.A., but I decided it's time for me to do something with my life. Not just because Dad always said so. Because I'm getting older."

"Okay. So what *are* you doing with your life?"

"I enrolled at your old alma mater."

"Really? Gunther Community College?"

"The very same. I'm just getting electives out of the way right now, but what I want to do is teach. Maybe they'll even set me up with a classroom at good old Gunther High."

I never expected Thom to be the one to end up in Gunther. I'd also never imagined Thom as a teacher, but at the same time, he did know how to command a room. Instead of a bunch of tipsy party people, he'd have a classroom full of kids for an audience.

"That's great, Thom." The conversation was finally buzzing along. "You still see Ronnie and John and Benji and Lindsay and everybody?"

"Not really. After you left, I was angry, and things between me and Jessa were a little weird. So I didn't go out much. And I stopped throwing parties."

"Sorry to hear that."

"It's not a bad thing. I guess you could say it forced me to focus."

"And are you and Jessa still friends?" They had known each other a long time. I hoped a lot of childish drama didn't ruin all that.

"Sure. When I saw how broken up she was after you left, it really sunk in that Jessa and I were never going to get together. I think that made it a lot easier for the two of us to be friends. Better ones, even, than we were before."

"Really." I thought about what Tim had said, about recording my own stuff. If I had been like Thom, and never tried to have some great romance with Jessa, maybe we would have just been friends like we should have been all along. Then we wouldn't have had to give up on those songs we wrote. "Is Jessa still playing music?"

"You haven't spoken to her?"

"No. Not at all."

"Interesting." Thom paused. "I guess I thought she would have called you by now."

"Why is that?"

"Well, a little while back I put her in touch with a guy I'd heard a lot about, but never actually met. Not a label guy. Just an L.A. exec with some spare cash. From what I hear, he wants to help Jessa record and release those songs you two wrote."

"Really." I let what Thom had just said sink in. I assumed that Jessa had given up on our songs, the same way I had. That, it seemed, was incorrect.

"Yeah. This guy—this investor—is the friend of a friend of an ex-girlfriend of mine. He's apparently been looking for the right indie project to take on for a long time. Jessa played him a few songs she recorded on her phone during one of your rehearsals, and he thought they had potential. That's all I know."

Friend of a friend. John had used the same words to describe Teresa. I guess that was just how people got things done in L.A. Through those unseen personal networks you could only break into if you spoke up, and asked the right person for a hand or a good word. "I guess Jessa needs my permission to use the songs, since we wrote them together."

"Probably."

I considered. "You know what? You can tell Jessa the songs are all hers. She can do whatever she wants with them. I wish her the best."

I didn't begrudge Jessa a shot at success. I wasn't angry, and I wasn't bitter. Not anymore. Anyway, I had my sights set on a different future. One I'd already begun.

Chapter 16

I hardly registered that Matt had been sending out applications at all, but in the summertime he received acceptance letters to UCal and UCLA. Despite UCal's offer of a full ride, Matt decided that UCLA's breezy, leafy campus was more his speed. In fact, the whole Westside was calling. He was tired of dirty downtown neighborhoods and the sound of sirens. He wanted the Los Angeles he had seen on postcards, with its palm-lined drives, fresh-faced girls, and landscaped lawns. He wanted an easy drive down Sunset to the beach—not a choking crawl on the polluted freeway.

Matt asked me to move into a Santa Monica bachelor pad with him—he almost expected it—but by then I had plans of my own. The apartment below Tim's (newly sans mold) was available, so I put in an application to rent it. Then I asked Teresa to move in with me. She had gone from show-buddy to girlfriend so easily, and so naturally, that I almost didn't notice it happening. But I was glad that it had. Teresa was my biggest supporter—not once did she protest my late nights in the studio—but she had her own life too.

As soon as we signed our lease, Teresa registered for music business classes at the Musician's Learning Institute. She didn't know what she wanted to do, but she knew she loved music more than anything—and she wanted to be ready when the right opportunity came along, whether that involved promoting concerts, booking at a venue, or managing a band.

~ ~ ~

The day we moved into our apartment, Teresa couldn't wipe the grin off her face. *Turpentine* couldn't have wiped it off. She was smiling big when we went to pick up the truck I reserved, and the whole time we spent packing it with boxes and furniture—most of which we had acquired from Dylan. After Teresa announced her new plans, he decided to move out of his efficiency and into his friend Jimmy's East Hollywood apartment.

After we finished carrying our possessions into our first-floor flat, Teresa and I stood outside what was now our building, staring at its peeling facade and the big wrought iron gate before us. The sunset had turned Hollywood into a moving painting executed in lavender hues. We both took a deep breath. Then we entered through the gate and stepped over the threshold of our new abode.

The apartment was Tim's in reverse, with a coat closet in the corner, a small kitchen, and a single bedroom. However, ours had been spared the unfortunate 1980s update that had been inflicted on Tim's place. The windows weren't new vinyl ones, but rows of small glass panels. The old pull-chain toilet was still intact. And everywhere we walked, hardwood squeaked under our shoes.

~ ~ ~

By the time Teresa and I finished socking away our possessions and tacking old records to the wall in interesting patterns, night had fallen and the sky had taken on the smoky orange-pink of urban nighttime. We retreated outside and let the warm air fill our lungs.

"You know, I'm going to be in the studio a lot. More than ever, now that Tim hired me on." When Tim found out I was moving to Hollywood, he promoted me from intern to engineer. The only stipulation? He wanted me to quit Pizza Kitchen and work for him full-time. "Are you going to be okay with that?"

Teresa squeezed my hand. "Of course. Greatness takes time. Anyway, my music classes start next week. Who knows? Maybe I'll be even busier than you are!"

With a grin, she got up, dusted off her black jeans, and hopped onto her skateboard. At the convenience store just south of our building, a couple of kids turned the corner abruptly, but Teresa was able to glide effortlessly around them. Her ease, and her steadiness, amazed me.

It was one of those magical nights where everything feels right in the universe. The lamps down on the Boulevard glowed like benevolent spirits and the potted palms outside our apartment building swayed with a breeze that I imagined brought good luck from afar.

For the first time, I had a distinct feeling that I was doing exactly what I was supposed to. That I had exactly the right person beside me.

~ ~ ~

After my move to Hollywood, I was in the studio every night. I had to be, just to keep up. Hollywood Death Star hadn't released their record yet, but they were happy with Tim's work, and word had spread. The projects just kept coming.

Of course, life in Hollywood wasn't all work and no play. Teresa was turning twenty-one, and Dylan had every intention of turning the occasion into an event. Specifically, he wanted all of us to go out to a supposedly exclusive dance club his old friend Parker claimed he would get us into free of charge.

At first, Teresa refused. Any form of dancing more athletic than headbanging was anathema to her. Then Dylan told her who was spinning. Apparently, Teresa had heard of the DJ. He was a big deal, and he played music she was into, and so Teresa had made an exception to her strict personal dancing ban.

A few minutes before Dylan's scheduled arrival, I was surprised to see Teresa slide on a dark, sleeveless top, step into a pair of ankle boots, and sweep her bangs to the side. She wasn't the type to dress up for anything, or anyone.

When Dylan showed up a few minutes later, he looked her up and down through the plastic-framed glasses I still hadn't pegged as necessity or accessory. "I'm impressed," he said.

Teresa scoffed. "What? You didn't think I could dress myself?"

I didn't admit that I was impressed too. It was obvious Teresa didn't want anyone to make a fuss. So I just kissed her on the top of the head and wished her another happy birthday as we stepped out into the warm Hollywood night.

In a parking lot behind the Boulevard, Teresa, Dylan, and I met Parker and Dylan's roommate Jimmy. Parker, rather than the carved-from-marble heartbreaker I'd pictured, was a smiley slip of a kid with stars tattooed in blue ink on his wrists. Jimmy was a punk with a head full of red liberty spikes.

"So, where is this place?" Teresa asked. There was no line. No velvet rope. No visible sign of a nightlife establishment at all, although I could feel the asphalt shake underneath my sneakers.

Dylan dropped his cigarette, crushed it under a boot, and turned his gaze toward Parker. "We'll follow you."

Parker nodded wordlessly, and Teresa, Jimmy, Dylan, and I trailed him across the parking lot, toward a metal door that looked more like it would lead into a walk-in refrigerator than a nightclub. When Dylan yanked it open, we all stepped into another world. And that world was at war.

The pounding music was up so loud I could feel the jelly in my eyes vibrating. All I could do was stand there gaping while a behemoth of a bouncer stuffed his hands into my pockets. Not being in possession of any chains or knives, I was quickly shoved along to a second stern-faced guard who put a hand out for my ID, flashed a light directly into my retinas, and waved me through.

Out on the floor, lasers skipped overhead and covered the sea of dancers in constantly morphing versions of war paint. I tried to calm myself with a deep breath, but only sucked a lot of searing fog into my sinuses. Fortunately, Teresa noticed me standing dumbly on the edge of the dance floor and grabbed my hand.

"This way!" she yelled. Then she dragged me over to a comically overstuffed couch covered with electric orange plush.

I would, of course, have been a hell of a lot more comfortable at a rock show in some dank but cozy underground venue than at a dance club. Still, I figured I could take a page from Jimmy's book. He looked completely out of place in a vest crudely stenciled with Johnny Rotten's face, and yet he was having a great time. While Dylan threw down some slick moves accompanied by a few understated spins, Jimmy did a swing dance so wild it parted the crowd.

Teresa and I howled at the show from our place on the couch until Dylan pulled Teresa to her feet and urged her toward the pulsing dance floor.

When she glanced back at me, I gestured for her to go. It was her twenty-first birthday. I wanted her to have a good time.

While Teresa danced with her friends, I got up and wandered toward the DJ booth, which was on a platform ten or twelve feet off the floor. The DJ inside spun, shuffled, and threw his long black hair back and forth.

I stood up against a pillar, listening, absorbing. The music was too energetic for me. Too flashy. Too frantic. I would have rather listened to Tim spin, but I did my best to appreciate the music for what it was. Music that made people move.

An hour later, Teresa appeared at my side, sweaty and wild-eyed. "How are you holding up?" she asked over the music.

"Just fine. Why?"

"This isn't your scene."

"Is it yours?"

"On the surface, no. I don't like the showoff, see-and-be-seen vibe. But behind the clothes, and the glamour, I can tell the people here really love this music. I don't know . . ." She shrugged, smiled. "Maybe this is even the kind of event I'd like to put together when I finish my degree."

"And the dancing?"

"I like it more than I thought I would. I just sort of let the music wash over me, and run all through me—and my body responded. It felt like the most natural thing in the world."

"So let's go back on the dance floor. I'll join you."

Teresa shook her head. "What I want is to spend the rest of my birthday night with you. At the apartment. Let's get out of here!"

"What will Dylan say about that?"

"Lawson. Dylan is dirty dancing with Parker as we speak. And how long has it been since we've had a few hours alone?"

That was all I needed to hear. I grabbed for Teresa's hand and we hurried across the dance floor, past the bouncers, and out onto the pavement. The club had been hot, airless. The atmosphere outside was cool, breezy, heavenly. We dodged nightclubbers and Hollywood's usual cast of shady characters. We wound through the backstreets. Then we were home.

Back at the apartment, I rushed to retrieve the bottle of champagne I had hidden in the back of the fridge, but I never got to pop the cork. By the time I swung into the living room, bottle held aloft, Teresa was snoring on the couch.

I chuckled softly. Teresa, who had always scoffed at the idea of nightclubs and dancing, had danced herself to exhaustion. As for me, I still had plenty of energy. Late nights had become the order of the day, and I often mixed until the wee hours while Tim was out spinning. If he needed me to tackle a new project, I would be only too glad to report for duty.

Quietly, I slipped into the bedroom to check for one of Tim's comically succinct text messages, always sent sans punctuation. Without bothering to turn on the light, I rolled over to the far side of the bed, grabbed my phone out of the charger on the windowsill, and swiped.

Right away, I saw there were no fresh messages. However, I had received a phone call. I frowned. That was unusual. Matt almost never called anymore, and Alli was unlikely to reach out so late. I clicked on my phone log, expecting to find I'd been the proud recipient of a sales call or some droning plea from a campaign robot.

I already had my thumb lifted, ready to swipe *delete*, but stopped short. When I took a look at the ten digits on the screen, I realized just how mistaken I was. The last number in my log was one I knew quite well. A number I'd dialed dozens of times.

I sat up, my pulse quickening. Jessa Warlow had called me, and it was no mistake. She would have had to ask someone—probably my brother—for my number. *But, why?*

All at once, my mind rewound, back to my last conversation with Thom. Jessa had found an investor. Some rich guy who wanted to help release our songs. She would want my permission to use our music. *Of course.*

That was no big deal. I always planned to give Jessa the go-ahead. I wasn't sure why I'd been seized with panic at the sight of her telephone number. There was no reason to dread a conversation with her, any more than there had been to have that first conversation with my brother.

I swiped to dial. It was late, but Jessa was a night owl—I knew that better than anybody. There was no reason to keep her, or her musical career, waiting.

After the third ring, I heard an audible intake of breath. "*Jesus.* Lawson."

"Jessa," I said, "it's been a while."

"Longer."

"You sound surprised to hear from me. You called me first, remember?"

"I didn't think you'd return my call."

"Why wouldn't I?"

"You know why, Lawson."

I did. But I had no interest in dredging up the ugly things that had transpired back in Gunther. I'd forgiven. Forgotten. Maybe more importantly, I'd moved on. "Thom says he helped you find an investor to release our music," I said. "A 'friend of a friend.' I assume that's what you want to talk to me about."

"Right. Yes." Jessa's voice gained in confidence. "After you left, I started searching for a label, for the right connection, for anything. Nothing materialized. Then, your brother and I started talking again. He made a few calls, and came back with the number for a certain Charlie Jackson."

"And he's already agreed to help you launch your career?"

"Yes. It was when I played him our songs. That's what decided it. Maybe," she said, "I should have asked you before I did that."

"It's okay," I said. "I would hate for the music we wrote to go to waste. I wish you the best of luck. I really do. And the songs? They're all yours."

"What do you mean, all yours?"

"I mean, go ahead. Record them. Release them. You don't even have to put my name in the credits."

Jessa paused. "Oh. That's what I thought. It seems we've had some sort of miscommunication, Lawson."

It was certainly starting to feel that way. "How so?"

"Well, Thom said you're an engineer at a studio. I hoped *you* would produce our music, Lawson. I guess I thought you might want to. Of course, if you're too busy . . ."

I cut her off. "I didn't say that." I took in a long, slow breath. It had never occurred to me that Jessa would want me to record our songs. Or that we might make music together again.

I closed my eyes. For the first time, I imagined how I would handle recording the songs Jessa and I had written back in Gunther. The settings I'd use. The sound I would want to achieve. In my head, I heard big, echoing beats. Acoustic strings plucked so clearly you'd swear they were being played in the room. Jessa's voice warm and gravelly on some tracks, soft and haunting on others.

Did I want to record our music? Yes, I did. Very badly. Now that I knew it was an option, I had to record and mix those songs. I needed to do them justice. Send them out into the world sounding like I knew they could, once I got my hands on them.

"There was a time when my boss gave me clearance to use the studio whenever I wanted, for my own project," I began. "That was back when I was an intern. When we didn't have quite so many projects. Let me talk to him. I'll find out if the offer still stands."

"Oh, Lawson," Jessa broke in. "You wouldn't be working pro bono. Charlie would pay your studio. The usual rates."

"He would really do that?"

"Absolutely."

"I have to be honest with you, Jessa. Tim and I do great work. We book a lot of bands. But we aren't exactly a name-brand studio."

"Doesn't matter. I already explained to Charlie that you know our music like nobody else."

"All right. And what about the distance? Is this Charlie guy going to fly you out here for a week or two?"

"Fly me? Well, no. I'm not in Gunther anymore."

"Really? Where are you?"

"I guess Thom didn't tell you."

"Tell me what?"

"I'm in Los Angeles, Law."

I heard what Jessa said, but it didn't compute. "What?"

"I'm in L.A."

"Right now?"

"Yes, Law. Right now."

"But . . . why? How?"

"Charlie convinced me that if I'm going to launch a music career, this is where I need to be. He even helped me get some freelance design work so I'd be able to pay rent."

I looked out the window. Outside, L.A. was a series of shapes in the darkness. Shadows over shadows over shadows. I tried to fathom that Jessa was out there somewhere, in the same city.

"Still there?" she asked.

I shook my head to clear it. I knew I'd have to see Jessa if we were going to record together. I knew I'd be working with her, in the same room. I just didn't realize how soon that would be.

I collected myself. "Yes, of course. If we're going to make a record—if an investor is going to pay for it—my boss Tim will want to know all the details. We should meet with him. Soon."

"Great," Jessa said, "you just tell me when, and where. And I'll be there."

When I hung up the phone, I slumped back against the pillows. I was looking forward to lying in the near dark for a little while, processing everything that had just happened.

However, just a few seconds later the room darkened, and I jerked out of my daze.

There, in the doorway, was Teresa. "Who should meet with Tim? Did you book a new band?" She yawned and smiled sleepily. "Sorry, I wasn't listening in. I just caught the tail end of your conversation."

I wished she hadn't. I hadn't even figured out how to explain what Jessa was to me. Ex-lover? Friend? Neither of those things seemed to matter.

"I was talking to an old songwriting partner," I said at last.

"Songwriting partner? Lawson, you never told me you had a *songwriting partner*. It sounds almost like you were in a band." Teresa climbed up next to me on the bed.

"I guess I was. Back in Gunther. We wrote nine or ten songs together."

"And he's in L.A. now? I can't believe you never told me any of this, Lawson." She clapped her hands. "I simply have to meet him!"

"*Her.* Her name is Jessa. Jessa Warlow. She was one of my brother's high school friends."

Teresa never wavered. "Jessa then. How long has she been here?"

"I'm not sure exactly. Not long."

"Does she know anybody? I mean, anybody who could take her out at night, or show her around?"

"I don't think so." I was pretty sure the guy who wanted to release our music didn't count. He was an executive, and probably an older guy. The kind who wanted to foot the bill for an indie music project because it would make him feel cool, or young, or relevant.

"Then let's welcome her—*Jessa*—to Los Angeles properly. You said she was in your brother's high school class? Well, then she'd be the same age as Lydia. I know there's business to be discussed, but I say we all take her out to dinner first—me, you, Tim, Lydia, maybe Dylan. We'll go someplace nice. Somewhere really L.A. We'll make it a party!"

Sometimes, Teresa had a way of getting ahead of herself. Making too big a deal of something that wasn't a big deal at all. This wasn't one of those times. I shrugged. "You know what? I think that's a great idea."

If I was going to work closely with Jessa, maybe even be holed up with her in the studio for a week or more, I wanted Teresa involved from the get-go. I wanted her to know Jessa, and understand completely that she was no threat to her, or to our relationship.

This time around, Jessa would be my bandmate, and maybe my friend. Nothing more. The way it always should have been.

Chapter 17

For Jessa's "welcome party," Teresa proposed an evening repast at Musso & Frank, a bar and grill with old Hollywood elegance and, occasionally, the smell of mothballs. Tim and Lydia agreed immediately. At first Dylan was not compelled to attend, but he changed his mind when Teresa promised to buy him dinner at an eatery more to his liking directly after. And so, at the appointed hour, Tim and Lydia met Teresa, Dylan, and I outside our building, and we walked a half mile of Hollywood's backstreets together.

When I pulled open Musso's heavy front door, letting the early evening sunshine light up the swirling dust, I caught sight of Jessa leaning against a wood partition near the host station in a red sweater dress and kitten heels. She fit in perfectly with the golden age glamour of Hollywood's oldest restaurant. I could have been looking at a photograph.

When the door closed behind me, plunging the vestibule into its usual gloom, I went to her. I thought it might feel strange, or at least a little disconcerting, to be in Jessa's presence once again. It didn't. All I felt was the warmth of friendship. The comfort of a familiar face.

I wasn't sure whether I should embrace Jessa, shake her hand, or maintain a dignified distance, but I never had to decide. Teresa reached Jessa before I did. She slipped past me and grabbed for Jessa's hands.

"You must be Jessa—the songwriter. I want to know all about the music you and Lawson wrote together! Of course I've always known he's a fantastic guitarist, but I didn't know until a few days ago that he's also a *composer*."

Jessa blinked, apparently taken aback at Teresa's exuberance, the way I had once been. "You'll just have let me know what you want to know."

"Everything, of course!"

"Hold on just a minute," I said with a laugh. "No one's even been officially introduced." Jessa was in a strange land, among strangers. I didn't want her overwhelmed before we even took our seats. "This is Teresa, my girlfriend, and her best friend Dylan."

Dylan cast his eyes over Jessa, but didn't make a peep. I ignored his rudeness and made room for Tim and Lydia, who stepped into place beside me. "This," I said, "is Tim, and his wife Lydia."

Jessa nodded. "A pleasure. I've heard a lot about both of you."

Lydia giggled and threw her arm over Tim's shoulder. "Only the most terrible and scandalous things, I hope."

Before I could say anymore, our host—an apparent centurion in red tails—appeared. He bowed, and our party followed him to a wooden booth by the bar.

As Tim slid into his seat, he pushed a business card Jessa's way. "If you or your investor want to look into my studio more closely, all the information is right here."

Jessa studied the card. "Very nice. If I'm not mistaken, this is professional work. Who's your designer?"

"Oh, that's me." Lydia shook her curls. "I have a degree in graphic design, but I'm working at a hotel, if you can believe it."

Jessa laughed. "I know how it is. Those dream jobs never seem to materialize for us art students. I have a degree in fine arts, but I'm mostly doing web updates. I don't even like computers. In fact, I despise them."

"You know, Teresa's in school right now," I broke in. "She's taking music business classes."

"Music business," Jessa repeated. "Now that sounds positively practical. What will you do with your degree?"

Teresa beamed at Jessa's attention. "I guess I'd like to be a concert promoter. Unless I find that one perfect band that I'd love to manage, and who wants to be managed by me. Then I'd give them my all."

"A band like Hollywood Death Star?" Lydia asked.

"Exactly!"

I couldn't believe how easily the conversation was flowing. The evening was already shaping up to be a success.

"So, you're from Chicago," Jessa was saying to Lydia. "How about you, Tim?"

"Believe it or not, I grew up in a small town two hours from Tucson. The kind where even the most upstanding residents spends their weekends shooting guns in T-shirts with cutoff sleeves."

Jessa smiled. "I take it you chose music over weaponry."

"Oh, the two aren't mutually exclusive. I have a pistol. With the equipment I keep in my apartment, it's practically a necessity. Not that I plan to 'pop any caps,' as they say. I figure all I have to do is point that sucker, and the thieves will turn tail."

Everybody at the table laughed except Dylan.

"Who is she again?" I heard him ask Teresa.

"One of Lawson's old friends," Teresa hissed. "I told you! They used to write music together back in Gunther."

I glanced to my left just in time to see Dylan raise an eyebrow. His expression was smug. "Do all of Lawson's 'old friends' look like that?"

Teresa rolled her eyes. "Oh, shut up, Dylan," she said.

I smiled to myself. I liked that Teresa hadn't taken Dylan's bait. She was too cool and secure to get jealous over Jessa, or anybody else I worked with in the studio. That was one more reason I knew Teresa was exactly the girl for me. As if I needed another.

~ ~ ~

After dinner, Teresa escorted Dylan off to one of the trendy ramen shops south of the Boulevard as she had promised. That left me, Tim, Lydia, and Jessa out on the street.

Night had fallen, but Hollywood was very much alive, its evening atmosphere best described as carnivalesque. Bright marquee lights chased each other atop Hollywood's tourist traps. The restless breeze, murmuring with the sounds of distant hubbub, was like the zephyrs stirred by roller coasters.

"Let's talk about your record," Tim said, arms crossed. "How are you going to do this?"

"What do you mean?" Jessa asked.

"I mean, I'm curious—is this recording going to be stripped down guitar and vocals? Are you going to hire a drummer? A whole band?"

Jessa looked at me. "I assumed it would just be the two of us and our guitars. But you're the producer, Lawson. What do you think we should do?"

I was hardly a producer, and only a few months in as a full-time engineer. Still, our songs played in my head, the same way they had the night Jessa told me she wanted me to record and mix our music. I heard our guitars over a slow, thudding beat. Jessa's voice rising to the front of the mix, with just a touch of delay.

"What I'd like to do is create beats with software, the way Tim does for a lot of the bands that come in to the studio." I shook my head. "I'm sure that's not what you were expecting me to say. I know it's something we've never considered. Never discussed."

Jessa nodded slowly. "You're right. That's not what I was expecting. But I'm intrigued."

"I could show you if you'd like."

"That won't be necessary." Jessa touched my wrist. "I trust you, Lawson. You know music, and you know our songs."

After Tim got the details about Charlie's involvement in our project, he and Lydia left Jessa and I alone. Lydia, "concierge extraordinaire," was due at the Franklin Hotel any minute.

"Law, I'm sure you know it," Jessa said, "but I'm really sorry for the way things happened between us back in Gunther."

"No apology necessary," I told her quickly. "It was a long time ago, and neither of us was in a good place back then. Please. Let's consider it water under the bridge."

Jessa smiled. "It's really good to hear you say that. I've missed making music with you, Lawson. Maybe even more than that, I miss being your friend."

I returned her smile. "Likewise."

~ ~ ~

Three nights later, Jessa met me at Tim's apartment for our first official recording session. I felt completely at ease sitting beside Jessa at Tim's desk. It was as if no time had passed at all—let alone seven months. As if we were just taking the next step with our music, and recording it like we'd always planned.

I opened up the program Tim favored and selected a file I had created in the days since our meeting at Musso. A slamming four-on-the-floor beat filled the room. It was a simple starter beat I'd created for the first song Jessa and I had written together, from scratch.

Jessa turned to me, chin cocked, guitar at the ready. "What do I do?"

"Play 'Estrella.' Jump in whenever you're comfortable."

Jessa took a deep breath and began to strum. In no time, she was locked into the beat. Clearly, she hadn't abandoned our songs the way I had. She wasn't rusty in the least.

When Jessa added her vocals, I shivered. I'd forgotten how full and warm her voice was. How it rattled with just a touch of gravel on the high notes. I had also forgotten just how *good* our songs were. All through the cold Gunther winter, Jessa and I had altered them and played them back over and over, making sure the flow was just right. The arc. The mood.

While Jessa strummed and sang, I made adjustments to the beat. I switched up the bass tone so it was even more thudding and added a ghostly echo to the snare. At first, I wasn't sure how to approach the toms, but I ended up dialing them back by removing a few hits from the loop.

By the time Jessa hit the bridge, I was just listening. Layered over the beat, her voice took on a haunting quality. The result really was just as I'd imagined. A strange, but synergistic juxtaposition.

After Jessa's last note, I hit the spacebar and halted the beat.

In the sudden silence, Jessa's eyes widened. "Lawson. I can hardly believe it. That was our song. But it was so much more." She shook her head.

"Should we try out a few more options? You know, keep searching for our sound?"

"*Searching for our sound?* Lawson, we just found it. Let's keep going. If you have another beat ready, that is."

I did. I'd stayed up the night before creating a beat for 'Ravens,' and another for 'Andromeda.'

By the time Jessa and I wrapped up our session, it was nearly midnight.

"Lydia's off early," Jessa said as she packed her guitar into its well-worn hard case. In Lydia's line off work, midnight was early. A normal shift ended just before dawn. "She texted earlier. She wants us to meet her and Tim at a place called Mel's."

"Ah. Mel's is a kitschy diner just down the street." One by one, I shut down the windows I had open on Tim's monitor. "You'll like it."

"I'm sure I will. But Lydia's invite is for the both of us." Jessa nudged my knee with the toe of her boot. "What do you say? Join us for fries and a nightcap?"

Since Teresa had decided she might want to promote electronic dance music events someday, she had been out almost every night with Dylan. That meant there was nothing waiting for me downstairs except two-day-old Chinese food and an empty living room.

I shrugged and grinned. "Wouldn't miss it for the world."

Chapter 18

Whenever we could find an hour or two, Jessa and I were locked in the studio, crafting beats. We tended toward a combination of pounding bass drum lines and reverb-heavy toms. When in doubt, we kept the beat sparse.

I wasn't sure if Charlie Jackson would really come through and "finance" our record. It was one thing to make promises to the pretty young graphic designer with the gravel-and-velvet voice. It was another to call up Tim, sign a contract, and make a deposit. But that, it seems, is exactly what Charlie did.

"Jessa's investor got in touch with me last night," he told me when I ran into him in the studio one morning. "Everything's in ink." Tim swiveled around. "I'd like you to consider this project your first priority, Law. From now until it's finished."

"Why's that?" I asked. "I mean, any special reason?" The last project Tim asked me to make first priority was the Hollywood Death Star record, and that was because HDS were indie darlings on the rise. Jessa and I didn't exactly match their status.

"Lawson. Charlie works at the new CX television network. The one that launched in the spring." He leaned back, fingers pressed together. "He's a vice president. Did you know that?"

"Sure, Jessa's mentioned it. But he isn't in the music department or anything. I think Charlie sells advertising. Or maybe he tells other people to sell advertising."

Tim shook his head. "Doesn't matter, Law. He's going to have connections. The kind that could lead to big business. Big contracts. Even licensing deals. We're starting to make a name for ourselves here in the local scene, but there's a whole world beyond that. If we're ever going to work somewhere that isn't my one-bedroom apartment—we have to get acquainted with that world." Tim looked at me pointedly. "Let's start," he said, "by impressing Charlie Jackson."

~ ~ ~

By the time Charlie had signed on the dotted line, Jessa and I were ready to move on to the part of recording I was most looking forward to—capturing our performances. I had already spent hours digging through Tim's collection of mics, new and vintage, searching for the perfect ones to capture our guitars and, of course, Jessa's voice.

"I'm nervous," Jessa said as she stood in the doorway, guitar case in hand, pressing one booted toe into the carpet. "Is that strange?"

"A little. You know our songs backwards and forwards."

"I guess it's different, when I know everything I'm playing could be the final version. The one that will be part of our record forever."

I stood. "So let's warm up together. The way we did back in Gunther, once we had all the kinks worked out."

Jessa nodded. "Another good idea, courtesy of Lawson Harper."

For our warm-up, we relocated to the roof of my building, a spot Tim often used to unwind after a long and grueling DJ gig. It was easiest to love Hollywood from three stories above it. The grime and the crime were firmly out of sight. There was just that restless Hollywood breeze, the green hills to the north, and in every other direction, the statues and spires that topped Hollywood's iconic buildings.

Up there on the roof, Jessa and I sat cross-legged on two of the chaise lounges someone had dragged up there long ago. We played song after song, the way we used to do. We were three thousand miles away from Jessa's bedroom, with its saffron carpet and golden lamplight, but it felt like old times.

I hardly noticed the passage of dusk to dark. When I finally looked up, Jessa's eyes were fixed on me. She grabbed for my wrist. "Lawson. Do you ever wonder what would have happened—what could have happened—if things hadn't gone so wrong in Gunther? If I hadn't been so stupid."

Jessa's distress disturbed me. We had just played beautifully, and I wanted her to be refreshed, feeling good, when we went back inside to lay down her guitar tracks.

"Don't think that way," I said, trying to lift her spirits. "I never would have come out here, or learned to record and mix. Considering where we are now, making a record with an investor footing the bill, I wouldn't change anything. Would you?"

"I don't know. It doesn't matter. Forget I said anything." She stood and gathered her coat around her. "Let's get started. I'm ready."

~ ~ ~

Because Teresa's opinion was so important to me, I asked her to wait to until I had a polished mix to listen to my music. In fact, I promised she would be the first to hear it. Before Tim. Before Thom or Allison. Before Charlie Jackson.

However, with Tim's apartment just above ours, it proved impossible to keep everything under wraps. One night, when Jessa headed downstairs for a quick leftover pad thai break, we found Teresa standing in the middle of the living room, seemingly mesmerized.

"Lawson," she said, "I didn't mean to listen. Dylan and I just stopped in for a minute. But just now, I could hear everything. Your music—it gave me shivers. I've never heard anything like it. I really think you've made something extraordinary." She turned to Dylan, who was posed in the corner of the couch. "Isn't that exactly what I said to you?"

He studied his nails and did everything he could to look bored. "I suppose it is."

Jessa grabbed my arm. "It's all because of Lawson. Sometimes I can't believe how talented he is."

I flushed.

Teresa beamed. "Me neither."

Dylan made a faint noise of disgust.

I didn't acknowledge Dylan's reaction, but I made a mental note to ask Teresa what was going on with Dylan. If I'd done something to offend him, I at least wanted to know what it was.

Chapter 19

Most of the time, I mixed alone. However, when Jessa wanted to sit in so she could give her input on the fly, I agreed. I was so comfortable with her that I didn't mind having her literally looking over my shoulder.

Every so often, Jessa and I retreated to Tim's couch to listen back to our work. I knew exactly what I was going for, on every track. I wanted the sound big, close, and intense. I wanted anyone listening to believe Jessa was right there beside them, whether she was whispering or belting in her wall-shaking voice. And I wanted the details handled artfully, rather than erased. I let a few of Jessa's in-breaths come through. In a few places, I highlighted the sound of my pick striking the strings.

On our fourth day of mixing, Jessa and I were camped out on the couch while the strains of our record poured from Tim's monitor speakers. When the last note of the last song sounded and faded away, I sat up swiftly. The sound was true, clear. Sections surged forward and pulled back exactly when I wanted them to. All the time, I could swear Jessa was singing next to my ear, when in reality she was huddled close to me on the couch, knees up, listening just as intently as I was.

"That's it, isn't it?" Jessa whispered. "We're finished!"

I nodded. "We have a draft."

"I can hardly believe it." Jessa threw her arms around my neck and held tight. "Finally, we have something to show for all our work."

Something, I thought, *good enough to change both of our lives.* But I didn't want to get ahead of myself.

"We should celebrate. We *must* celebrate." Jessa got to her feet. "I'll go see Lydia at the Franklin. She'll fake sick. And where is Tim? Recording drums? Lydia will make him cut out early!"

"I'll go downstairs and catch Teresa and Dylan before they head out for the night."

I also planned to make good on my promise that Teresa would be the first to hear my polished mixes. While Jessa set out for the Franklin Hotel, I sat down at Tim's desk, bounced down the record, and saved it to one of the flash drives Tim kept handy. Then I raced downstairs.

When Teresa saw me in the doorway, panting and holding one of Tim's flash drives aloft, she knew exactly what that meant. "Lawson, no. It can't be! You didn't even tell me you were close."

In three seconds, she reached me. In five, she had the flash drive plugged into her tablet, headphones on her ears, and her eyes closed. Dylan, who was curled on the couch playing with his phone, was all but forgotten.

When the first song finished, Teresa moved toward me wordlessly and wrapped her arms around my middle. "It's amazing," she said into my sweatshirt.

She pulled back and gazed up at me. "I mean it, I'm amazed! The beats are huge, Lawson. This song sounds like it was recorded in a music hall, not Tim's little apartment."

Teresa didn't play an instrument, and she couldn't sing. And yet she understood music better than anybody else I knew. I broke into a grin.

Just as Teresa began sliding my headphones back over her ears, Dylan gave a little cough to remind her that he was still in the room.

She clapped a hand over her mouth. "Dylan! I'm sorry. It's just . . . you have to hear this!"

"What is it?" he asked cautiously.

"It's Lawson's record, of course. The one he wrote and recorded and mixed."

"Right." Dylan looked like he had just smelled something bad. He sniffed and turned away. "With that guitar girl."

"Yes. With the 'guitar girl.' *Jessa*."

I let Dylan off the hook. "It's okay. There will be plenty of time to listen to the record. Jessa thinks we should celebrate, and I agree. Both of you—come out with us to Mel's. Drinks are on me."

"I don't think so," Dylan said. "In fact, I'm going to head home."

Teresa's eyes zoomed his way. "Why? We practically just got here."

"And now," he said, "I'm practically just leaving." Without another word, Dylan zipped up his jacket and let himself out.

I raised an eyebrow in what I can only describe as complete astonishment. "What was that? Is something bothering him?"

Teresa shook her head. "Let's not talk about Dylan right now. This is your night. Let's get down to Mel's. Let's have a good time!"

~ ~ ~

Twenty minutes later, all the people who meant the most to me were situated around what had become "our booth."

"The usual?" asked our server, a ponytailed actress–waitress who had taken care of us many times before.

"The usual," I confirmed, and in no time, a triple order of fries and gravy graced our chrome table. Two pitchers glinted in its shiny center.

Teresa tilted her chin. "It's almost like you're all regulars," she said.

I hadn't thought about it before, but we really were. Whenever Lydia could get away, Tim, Jessa, and I met her at Mel's Drive-In, her favorite Hollywood eatery.

While I filled up beer glasses for me and Teresa, Tim pointed a fork in my direction. "You've done good work, Lawson. That old condenser you chose for vocals brought out some killer tones. Everything sits together just like it should. Now it's time to get that draft to Charlie. You know you'll need to incorporate his feedback before you master."

I nodded. "I'll send him a link."

"Oh," Jessa said, "don't."

"Why not?"

"I suppose I forgot to mention. Charlie wants to meet you. He asked that we bring our tracks by in person. What do you say?"

"I say 'excellent.' I can't wait to make the acquaintance of our great benefactor."

Tim slapped me on the back. "Good man! That's what I like to hear." He glanced at Lydia.

"Now all *that's* decided," Lydia broke in, "I propose that we talk about something besides work!" Lydia leaned her arms on the table. "I'll start. We're having a party! A Christmas party. For Hollywood orphans. You're all invited."

Jessa arched an eyebrow. "Orphans?"

"As in Los Angelenos with no family in the city. Destined to spend Christmas alone."

"Aren't you a native?" Tim asked Teresa.

"Sure. But my parents are assholes."

Lydia giggled. "So that settles it! We'll all be there, and so will Tim's old roommates, and some of the girls from the hotel."

All through the rest of the evening, Lydia had her wish. There was no more talk about business, or the studio, or the record. We were all better for it. It turned out to be one of those really great nights, where everybody is getting along and everybody's having a good time.

Even the wait staff seemed to feed off our good vibes. When we'd polished off our pitchers, our server sent over two more, free of charge.

~ ~ ~

Back at the apartment, I finally had the opportunity to open up the bottle of champagne I bought for Teresa's birthday. While I popped the cork and filled two short water tumblers with champagne, Teresa put on music—something low-key, that mostly consisted of video-game style blips.

After I passed Teresa her glass, she sunk into the couch. "I'm so glad I didn't go out dancing tonight. I needed this. Time with you. *A rest.* Sometimes I can't keep up with Dylan."

I settled in next to Teresa. I would also, at long last, have the chance to ask what had prompted Dylan's apparent aversion to my very presence. "Why did he cut out of here so fast anyway?"

"You know Dylan . . ."

"Yes, I know Dylan can be moody, but I've never seen him walk out. Or turn down a free drink. I'm starting to wonder what exactly he's got against me."

"Oh, it isn't you, Law."

"Then what is it?"

Teresa gazed up at me from under her row of straight black bangs. "It's Jessa." She shrugged. "Dylan doesn't like her."

I laughed in surprise. "*Jessa?* Really? What could he possibly have against her?"

"Are you sure you want to know?"

"Of course."

"Okay. Well, Dylan's convinced Jessa wants you. He thinks she's got it bad."

"What?" I laughed. "That's ridiculous."

"I know. Dylan is so much drama." Teresa took a gulp of champagne and grinned. "What can I say? It keeps life interesting."

"What gave him that idea?"

Teresa twirled her glass in her hand. "I guess he just thinks it's a little over the top, the way she's always gushing about you. About how talented you are and everything."

"Is that all?"

"He also thinks it's kind of *bold*, the way she'll take your arm, or play with your fingers, right in front of me. I told him if she meant anything by it, she'd wait to do that in private."

"We're very comfortable with each other. We've known each other a long time."

"That's what I told Dylan. He won't listen."

I sat back against the couch. Something Jessa said while we were warming up on the roof was coming back to me. *Do you ever wonder what would have happened—what could have happened—if things hadn't gone so wrong in Gunther?* I wondered if, just maybe, I hadn't caught her full meaning. I wondered if, maybe . . .

I shook my head. What I was beginning to think was crazy. Outlandish. Impossible.

"This has been going on for a while," Teresa went on. "Dylan never bought the 'old friends' thing." Teresa wiggled her eyebrows. "He's sure you used to get hot and horny back in old Gunther, P.A."

"Oh."

"I know." Teresa rolled her eyes. "Stupid, right?"

Suddenly, I felt light-headed. Even feverish. The room spun. I wished I could agree with Teresa, but that, of course, would be a lie.

Teresa nudged me. "Hey. You okay? Did Dylan rain all over your parade?"

He had, but not in the way Teresa thought. I had never actively decided to hide my history with Jessa. I simply wrote it off as irrelevant. Now, Dylan had made a wild guess and landed on the truth. My innocent omission, by default, became a sordid secret. The kind that could make trouble in my relationship with Teresa. Or even blast it apart.

I turned to Teresa. "There's something I should tell you."

Her smile faded. "Something like what? You're making me nervous, Lawson."

There was only one way to diffuse an explosive secret. And that was to tell it—no matter how uncomfortable it was.

"When Jessa and I first reconnected in Gunther, we were both lonely. Confused. We tried being more than friends, and bandmates at the same time. Needless to say, it didn't work out."

Teresa leaned forward and turned off the music. "Lawson. You're just telling me this now?"

"I wish I told you sooner."

"So why didn't you?"

"Because it was very brief, and a mistake."

Teresa's eyes fixed on the coffee table. "I just never seriously considered it—you and Jessa. You seem so different from each other. She seems so much older. Now I don't know what to think. You're locked up there in the studio with her almost every night. You're out with her on the Boulevard."

"It wouldn't matter how often we were together. I don't even see Jessa that way anymore. I couldn't if I tried."

Teresa peeled her gaze off the coffee table. "How do you expect me not to worry? Knowing that you two used to . . ."

I looked away. "We all have a past."

"Of course."

"I guess I just need you to trust me. That you're the one I want to be with." I set down my drink. "If I've caused you to doubt me, I'll change. Please. Tell me what I can do."

"We don't see much of each other anymore."

"I can't deny that."

"I guess it's easy for me to imagine us drifting apart. And then, if Dylan's right . . . Jessa will be right there, waiting."

"He isn't right. All those nights I spent with Jessa in the studio, she's been nothing but the consummate professional. But that doesn't mean I can't make more time for us to be together."

"How? When?"

"Whenever I can get away from the studio, I'll do what you do. If you're going out—I go, too."

"You would really do that?"

I understood why Teresa was skeptical. She knew I didn't like trendy Hollywood dance clubs. She knew I didn't want to take a night away from the studio. But, for Teresa—and for what we had—I figured I'd go just about any place. Anytime.

"I really would," I told her. "And I will."

Chapter 20

I meant what I said to Teresa. I was going to make time for her. I was going to suck it up and go to a see-and-be-seen dance club whenever I could get away from the studio. But first, it was time for me to meet Charlie Jackson.

No longer would he be a mythical creature or some god on high functioning somewhere in the background of my life. He would be a real person, whose hand I had shaken. With whom I had broken bread.

I pictured Charlie as an older gentleman, with a pin-striped suit and one of those baby-kisser smiles. I could not have been more wrong. When I arrived at Jessa's place on the night of our scheduled meeting, I found a fit thirty-something with smooth, dark skin, hair cut close to his head, and a pair of steely eyes. He paced the room, making Jessa's modestly-sized North Hollywood apartment feel half its size.

"You must be Lawson," Charlie said before I could speak. When he extended his hand, I prepared myself for one of those digit-crushing power shakes, but he only delivered a civilized pump.

"I know Jessa's quite pleased with the work you've done," Charlie went on. "Of course I'm very interested in hearing this record for myself."

Jessa and I were all set. She'd already loaded the songs into her phone and synched it to the portable speaker I'd borrowed from the studio.

Before she could press *play*, Charlie held up his keys and flicked them so they jingled. "Actually, I'd like to go for a ride."

Jessa laughed and tossed her hair, the way she did when she was nervous. "What are you talking about, Charlie?"

"I just got a brand new sound system. So . . ." He pushed open the apartment door, then glanced over his shoulder. "Let's take a ride."

~ ~ ~

What's big on style, low on legroom, and costs more than most people make in a year? Charlie Jackson's car, of course. As soon as Jessa locked up, Charlie pressed a button on his key fob and the spiffy little BMW parked next to the curb let out a chirp.

After Charlie opened up the passenger side door and bent the seat forward, he shot me an apologetic glance. "Sorry, Lawson. According to the laws of chivalry, ladies must ride shotgun."

"Understood." I slid into the back and smashed my knees up while Charlie and Jessa slid into the bucket seats up front.

I had barely buckled up when the car roared to life. Having become accustomed to reliable sedans with automatic transmissions, being a passenger in that powerful car felt like riding the back of a monster. Charlie's average speed turned out to be breakneck. Save for my seatbelt, I would have been pitched to the far side of the car with every turn.

The front seat, it seemed, provided a smoother ride. After Jessa handed Charlie her phone, he was able to sync it up with his sound system without taking his left hand off the wheel.

After a few nervous seconds, the first notes vibrated through the car—and I quickly forgot about the bumpy ride. The sound came through even bigger and warmer than it did through Tim's monitors. Clearly, Charlie had shelled out for a top-of-the-line sound system. The effect was dazzling, and it was not lost on Jessa. She turned around. When she saw my helpless grin, she leaned back and linked her fingers with mine.

Charlie, however, was not so easy to read. His face didn't change the whole time we were on the 170, or when we eased onto Ventura. Even after he pulled very suddenly into an empty space, he only stared intensely at the steering wheel.

"Charlie!" Jessa practically yelled. "What do you think?"

After a few more suspenseful seconds, he spoke up. "It's good," he said slowly. "Maybe really good. Certainly much better than I was expecting. When you told me about those electronic drums, I figured I was going to have to send you back in the studio with a real drummer. But the beats are working." He paused, as if searching for the right words. "In fact, I think that's what makes your sound really unique. Of course I don't have to tell you the singing is fantastic. Or this guitar work." He glanced at me in the rearview mirror. "How long have you been playing, Lawson?"

"Since I was nine."

He nodded. "It shows."

Jessa put a hand on Charlie's wrist. "What happens next?"

He killed the engine. "We grab a bite to eat. The three of us have a lot to talk about."

~ ~ ~

I had the impression that Charlie had simply nosed into the first available spot along Ventura so he could gather his thoughts. That wasn't the case. He beckoned Jessa and I to follow him, and we hustled to keep up while he proceeded at a brisk clip a half block west. I didn't notice the door all covered with ivy until Charlie pushed it open.

"We're here," he said, as we all stepped into a grotto full of blazing fireplaces and trees wrapped with twinkle lights.

A hostess dressed in sleek black placed us at a low, lounge-style table strewn with candles. As soon as we got comfortable, Charlie ordered a round of fancified pub fare for the table. Then he let us in on what he was thinking.

"Part of the fun of sending you two off with this project was that I really didn't know what to expect," he said. "Like I said, I really am impressed. I only have a few suggestions. Once those final changes are made, I'll have the record mastered at a different studio—from what I understand, that is the protocol for a serious recording."

Charlie was clearly enjoying his little pet project. When it came to the record-making process, he'd done his homework. However, our night out also gave me another insight into Charlie's motivations. He was in love with Jessa.

Those flashing eyes of his softened whenever he glanced her way, and he always seemed incredibly pleased with himself whenever he could draw out a laugh. By that time, I was so used to being Jessa's friend and bandmate that sometimes I forgot she was very beautiful. That she was the kind of woman men like Charlie would chase in the subtle, unhurried way they reserved for girls they might like to wife up someday.

I figured Charlie would try to turn the evening into your classic wine-and-dine. Those fireplaces certainly provided the mood lighting. But after we'd polished off our meal, Charlie simply paid the bill and thanked our server. On the way out, he handed me a small square of paper containing his feedback on the record.

I had no idea he had even taken written notes. I had no idea he *could* take notes while driving at a death-defying pace in his unwieldy vehicle, but there they were. Charlie was specific as to where he wanted the changes he'd requested— he had written down the exact time in the three songs in question—but the actual instructions were rather vague.

"Must be BIGGER," he'd marked down in regard to one section. "Needs something," he'd jotted in another.

I wasn't sure exactly what Charlie wanted, let alone how to deliver, but I wasn't worried. I was simply going to do what countless audio engineers before me had done. Sleep on it.

Chapter 21

When I got home, Teresa was in the bathroom getting ready. I joined her at the mirror. While she applied liquid liner, I threw on a fresh T-shirt and combed my hair.

Teresa's eyes slid left. "Lawson, what are you doing?"

I grinned into the cloudy mirror. "Whatever you're doing."

She brightened. "Really? You're coming out tonight?"

"If you want me to."

"Of course I want you to! You won't have to worry about cover either. Parker knows the bartender at a club on the Boulevard called Epitome. We'll all get in for free."

"For someone who doesn't say two words, Parker sure knows a lot of people."

Teresa smiled. "It's one of the great mysteries of our time." Then she pulled off her T-shirt and slipped into a black sheath dress I'd never seen before. The fabric draped over her shoulder blades, revealing the pale skin down to the small of her back.

"A dress?"

She shrugged. "I thought I'd try something new."

All I could do was stand back and admire. I knew Teresa didn't think of herself as beautiful, but with her pale skin and large amber eyes, there were moments when she looked positively otherworldly.

~ ~ ~

As it turned out, Epitome was one of those nightclubs in which patrons are made to wait outside in the biting evening air behind a velvet rope. Teresa, Dylan, Parker, and I, however, were spared that indignity because of Parker's connection.

After the expected manhandling by security staff, we made it inside the club, which was darker and danker than the club we'd visited on Teresa's birthday. There were no brightly colored lasers. Just fog and chandeliers made out of what appeared to be machine parts.

Immediately, Parker led us all to the bar, which stretched from one end of the room to the other. All of the bartenders wore the same mesh shirts and tight vests. When one particularly well-built bartender saw Parker, he hurried in our direction.

The way the bartender leaned over the bar, and the way Parker got up on his tiptoes so he could whisper something in his ear, made it immediately obvious that they were more than friends.

Teresa acted quickly. She stepped in front of Dylan to block his view. "Your eyeliner," she said, "it's smudged."

He made a sound of annoyance and turned his glasses around to try to get a look at his reflection. "Already? Why does that always happen on nights that are really important to me?" he whined.

"Don't worry," Teresa said soothingly, "we'll fix it. I have a cadet blue pencil in my purse that's a perfect match. *Aseo pronto!*"

With that, I followed Teresa and Dylan across the floor and through a squat concrete entrance that I only pegged as a unisex bathroom when I was already inside. Clubgoers, male and female, moved from stall to sink, and then back out onto the dance floor, in an ever-flowing stream.

The three of us headed for a few sinks in the darkest corner of the room that were not in use. While Teresa removed her makeup from the tiny purse she used on club nights and Dylan produced a comb from his back pocket, I leaned back against the nearest wall. Like all the others, it was raw concrete and spray painted with vulgar sayings that might have been graffiti, or some kind of decoration.

In front of the circular mirrors hung over each sink, Teresa re-applied her eyeliner and Dylan fixed his part. After a few seconds of primping they traded implements. Teresa availed herself of Dylan's comb and he added a little liner under his eyes. Then—very casually—Dylan pulled out a compact, flipped it open, and sucked some powder up his nose.

I pretended not to notice. What Dylan did was no business of mine. But, while I leaned against the wall and listened to the jarring cacophony of toilets endlessly flushing, Dylan nudged Teresa. She brushed him off, but he shot her an exasperated glance and pushed the compact in her direction. Nobody had to explain to me what that meant. Teresa would have partaken if I wasn't there. Probably had, on many occasions.

Before I could decide what I thought about that, Dylan rolled his eyes and caught Teresa with his elbow. Appearing to give in, she grabbed the compact out of his hand, sucked its remaining contents into her nasal cavity, and scraped the back of her hand against her nose.

I frowned.

"Please don't make a big deal, Lawson," Teresa said, under her breath. Then she collected her makeup and stuffed it into her miniature purse. "It's just something we do when we go out. It's something *everyone* here does. Okay?"

I blinked. "Was that . . . was it cocaine?"

Dylan snickered.

Even Teresa couldn't completely suppress a smile. "Well, it's not the 1980s, Lawson."

While I struggled for something to say, Dylan smirked his most Dylanesque smirk, pivoted on one booted foot, and left me and Teresa alone.

"I wish you would stop looking at me like that, Lawson," Teresa said as she pushed her hands under the faucet and cleaned a few traces of makeup from her fingers. The green bulbs above the mirror bathed her face, and the running water, in an alien light.

"Like what?"

"Like you're judging me." She grabbed a paper towel from the dispenser on the wall right next to me. "I think," she added, "you're the last one who should be judging anybody."

"What does that mean?"

"Well." She crumpled up the paper towel in her fist and tossed it into the trash without meeting my eyes. "For one, I put up with a lot more than most girlfriends ever have to. You've spent practically every night for the last six weeks locked up in the studio with your ex. Even if you weren't doing anything, who knows what you were thinking? *Remembering?*"

"Teresa. You know I don't think of Jessa that way. I couldn't even if I wanted to."

She whirled around. "I'm really supposed to believe that?"

"Yes. Because it's true."

Teresa's face hardened. "I don't know, Law. Pretty hard to believe considering you used to put it in her."

I flinched. "I wish you wouldn't talk that way."

Teresa rolled her eyes. "Oh, I've hurt Law Harper's sensitive sensibilities. Sometimes I think it has to be an act, the way you play so innocent. You live in L.A., but a dance club is just *too overwhelming* for you. You work in the music business, but you're still shocked by party drugs. The only thing I know for sure is how good you are at sucking the fun right out of any room. Like a goddamn Hoover."

I looked at Teresa in the mirror. Her skin was green and sickly in the bathroom's strange lighting. Her eyes, usually approaching amber, were black and empty. "Is that really what you think about me?"

"That's what everybody thinks about you, Lawson. You really believe Dylan was happy when I said you were tagging along?"

I turned away. "I guess I'll go," I said.

"I think," she said, "you should."

She didn't have to tell me twice. I got the hell out of that bunker-style bathroom and moved through the club toward the door—shoving when I had to—then stumbled out onto the street.

The whole way down the Boulevard and up Highland, all I could think was that it had to be the drugs. The way Teresa had spoken to me wasn't the way we spoke to each other. The Teresa I had seen in that bathroom wasn't the Teresa I knew. Or at least I hoped it wasn't.

When I got back to the apartment, my adrenaline was still surging. I laid down, but my blood wouldn't stop rushing through my veins and throbbing in my temples. Finally, I got up and took a couple of sleeping pills from a box I kept on hand in case I needed them after a long night in the studio. They were just over-the-counter shit—the same stuff my mother had used for years—but they did the trick. After swallowing a few pills dry, I shut the blinds, threw the covers over my head, and I was out.

~ ~ ~

In the morning, Teresa grabbed my shoulder through the covers to wake me. I could see little points of her hair, and the shades of her skin, through the tiny holes in the blanket. "Lawson," she hissed. "Please talk to me. I'm so sorry."

I turned over. I wasn't ready to face Teresa. I wasn't ready to rehash the previous evening, or make heavy decisions about what it meant for our relationship, or my life. I wanted to be left alone.

Instead of slinking away after my obvious rebuff, Teresa grabbed my arm. "Lawson!" she said again. "*Please.*"

With a sigh, I tossed the covers aside. To my incredible relief, I didn't see the scowling creature that had sneered at me in a bathroom covered with ugly sayings meant to pass as art. I saw my girlfriend. In one of my clean white undershirts. Looking fresh and sweet—and sorry—in the morning sunlight.

"I can't believe the way I acted last night," she whispered. "Can you ever forgive me?"

"I don't know." I sat up and scooted back against the headboard. It's just . . . what happened last night? Was it the drugs?"

Teresa shook her head. "I wish I could blame the way I acted on drugs, Lawson. The truth is, my jealousy got the best of me."

"Jealousy?"

"I'm jealous, Law. I don't like admitting it. But I am. I'm jealous of what you and Jessa used to have. I'm jealous because she's so beautiful. I'm jealous because you'll always have your music. I know you think I shouldn't be . . ."

I pressed back against the headboard. "But you are."

"Yes. I am."

"Okay." I took a deep breath and let myself absorb what Teresa had just said. The more it sunk in, the more it made sense. I had dumped my whole history with Jessa on Teresa, like it was nothing. To me, that's all it was. But to Teresa, it was much more. "Maybe," I said, "I should be apologizing to you."

"No, Lawson. You didn't do anything wrong. You told me the truth."

"And then I disappeared back into the studio. I left you to deal with it on your own."

"Still, I have no excuse for the things I said."

"You only lashed out at me because you were hurting."

Teresa sucked in air. "Does that mean you forgive me?"

I took Teresa's hand. "Of course I forgive you."

"Oh, thank god." Teresa breathed a long, ragged sigh of relief. "I'll never be unkind to you again, Lawson." She threw her arms around my neck. "I swear it. Really . . . I swear it!"

Chapter 22

On Christmas Eve I decided to do something I hadn't done since I left Gunther—I set up a tree. It wasn't that I had changed my mind about my least favorite holiday—I just wanted to show Teresa I was trying. And that there were no hard feelings about a certain unpleasant exchange in a nightclub bathroom.

After Teresa went to bed on Christmas Eve I slipped outside, dragged in a potted palm from the courtyard, and trimmed it with convenience store candy canes and tinsel. Underneath, I arranged a few gifts I'd surreptitiously procured on the Boulevard and hidden under the bed next to my guitar.

I made sure to sneak out of bed early so I could see Teresa's face when she emerged from the bedroom, and the payoff was everything I hoped it would be.

After a few sleepy steps, Teresa stopped dead. Then she rubbed her eyes, as if she might be dreaming. "Lawson! What is this?"

"It's for you."

"But, Lawson . . . you hate Christmas."

"Untrue." I grinned. "In fact, I may well be the jolliest motherfucker in all of Hollywood."

At my urging, Teresa opened her gifts, which consisted of a record player with state-of-the-art speakers, a stack of old records, and a fully intact Hungry Hungry Hippos game—a lucky vintage store score. The record player, of course, was the main attraction. Teresa couldn't wait to try it out, so we set 'er up, plugged 'er in, and then selected an Elvis Christmas album for its inaugural musical voyage.

The vinyl was scratched, so Elvis creaked as much as he crooned, but we both agreed our little apartment had never felt so festive.

~ ~ ~

When afternoon rolled around, Teresa and I linked arms and headed up to Tim's apartment. I couldn't wait to be part of one of Tim's Hollywood Orphans parties for the very first time, and I had never been so glad to have Teresa at my side. My only worry was Teresa existing in the same space as Jessa, and that worry was quickly put to rest.

As soon as Teresa and I stepped into the living room, Jessa waved from the kitchen, where she was helping Lydia prepare some exotic *hors d'oeuvres*. Immediately, I looked at Teresa to check her reaction. She smiled warmly and waved back. Then she squeezed my arm, letting me know that everything was going to be okay. That she could be around Jessa, no problem. That there was no bad blood.

After I grabbed a couple of champagnes from the card table set up in the corner, Tim introduced me to some of his old roommates as his "right hand man." Then Brian from Hollywood Death Star arrived.

"How's it going?" Tim asked. "Any plans for releasing the record?"

Brian pushed back his thinning hair, then let is spring back into place. "We've got a few indie labels fighting over it, actually."

Tim clicked his champagne glass against Brian's. "That's good news for all of us!"

Brian nodded. "When the smoke clears, I think we're going to have a pretty good deal. We're still not on the radar of any majors, but we don't want to risk getting signed and then shelved anyhow."

"Good thinking," Tim said. "Wait for the majors to get wind of your sales, and let them buy you out."

As much as I wanted to hear about what was happening with the HDS record, I didn't want to bore Teresa with too much shop talk. "Let's get some more champagne," I whispered.

"Yes," she said, holding up her empty glass, "let's!"

Before we'd gone two steps, one of Lydia's work friends fingered the hem of her dress and asked, "Where'd you get this?"

"Iguana. On the Boulevard. Have you been?"

I could tell she was glad to have somebody to talk to. So she felt like a real guest instead of my plus-one. I touched Teresa's shoulder. "I'll get our refills," I told her quietly.

She nodded and continued her conversation.

Meanwhile, I wove through a group of Tim's old roommates, who he'd lived with six to a room on Venice Beach, and then sidled up to the card table where Tim had parked the champagne. As I scooted in from the left, Jessa scooted in from the right with a fresh tray of fancy finger foods.

"Hey!" She put a hand on my wrist. "Lawson. I've been meaning to tell you. I got you something."

"Oh. Really?" I glanced around, searching for Teresa, but she was out of view. "I didn't think we were exchanging."

"We're not. It's just something I want you to have." Jessa's eyes sparkled. "Can you spare a moment now? Or would you rather I wait till later?"

I hesitated. For some reason, I had the feeling I was doing something I wasn't supposed to. At the same time, that seemed silly. Teresa and I had talked out our problems. She'd indicated that her jealousy was under control. "I guess it will have to be now," I said finally. "Teresa's friends are coming by in half an hour."

Jessa clapped her hands together. "Well, this won't take long. Sit down, won't you?"

"Uh. Sure." I sat down heavily in Tim's easy chair, which was shoved up against the wall behind me.

When Jessa opened up Tim's closet and removed a guitar case, I figured she was just moving it out of the way. Then she hefted it into my lap.

I looked at the hard case, dumbstruck. "This?"

"Yes, this. Open it!"

What else could I do? I unlatched the lid of the black hard case and lifted it high. Inside, I found the most beautiful electric–acoustic guitar I'd ever seen in my life. The shining wood was inlaid with mother-of-pearl and all of it was polished to a sleek shine. When I ran my hand down the neck a little shiver wormed its way down my spine.

I peered at Jessa in disbelief.

"I want you to use it on the record," she said. "Charlie told me about the note he wrote you. About the spots where something was missing. I don't think we need to add anything. I think we just need a different *sound*."

"I can't take it," I told her. But I was already lifting the guitar out of the case. I couldn't resist. I strummed a few times. The sound was stunning and it wasn't even perfectly in tune. When I tightened a few strings and played a single chord, the notes rang in my ears, so big and vibrant that they startled me.

By then, Tim had noticed the guitar that was gleaming in my lap. He made his way over and whistled. "Check this out," he said, "it's a beaut."

"Yes, it is a beaut," I agreed. Even though I had never used the word "beaut" in my life.

Just then, Teresa appeared at my elbow. "What's this?" she asked.

"A gift. From Jessa." I lifted my guitar into her arms.

For a moment Teresa held it uncertainly, like a distant relative's baby. Then she relaxed and strummed a couple of the chords I'd shown her.

"It's nice," she said finally. "You deserve something like this, Law. I know you'd never buy it for yourself."

~ ~ ~

When Teresa and I left Tim's soiree, it was our turn to play host. By half past six, Teresa, Dylan, Jimmy, and Jimmy's new girlfriend were all cozied up on the couch, passing around a bottle of Jim Beam. Elvis was back on the record player, and Parker and I were on the floor, locked in a tense game of Hungry Hungry Hippos.

I was having a great time, and as far as I could tell, everybody else was, too. As much as I enjoyed associating with Tim's friends and sampling fancy *hors d'oeuvres*, there was something charming—even comforting—about drinking liquor straight out of the bottle and playing a children's game. As far as I was concerned, I was having the best Christmas I'd ever had, and I was sure nothing in the world could interfere with my pleasant whiskey buzz.

That is, until Teresa and Dylan defected from the couch and took up position against the wall. I don't know why it bothered me . . . but it did. "Hey, Teresa, why don't you stick with the rest of us?" I called. "You're making me nervous with all that hush-hush stuff."

"Nothing's hush-hush, Law," Teresa called back.

"Then why all the low talk?"

"If you must know, we're *discussing* the guitar Jessa gave to you," she answered.

"What about it?"

"Jimmy just told me guitars like that cost more than a thousand dollars. Did you know that?"

I shrugged. "It was a gift. I don't need to know what it

cost," I said without looking up from the game in front of me. Parker played a mean game of Hungry Hungry Hippos.

"You don't think that's weird? That Jessa would spend that much money on a Christmas present."

"It's more than a Christmas present. Jessa wants me to use that guitar on the record."

"Well, I think it's pretty unbelievable."

I wasn't interested in a fight. Especially since everything had been copacetic five minutes ago. So I kept quiet and, after Parker beat me handily, challenged him to a rematch.

"Lawson!" Teresa yelled over the sound of munching hippos. "She spent more than a *thousand dollars.* You really don't have anything to say about that?"

"All I have to say is that everything was going fine until Dylan started whispering in your ear."

"This isn't about Dylan, Lawson."

"Then what's it about?"

Teresa stood, fists balled up at her sides. "It's about all of them, taking you away from me! Am I supposed to just sit back and let it happen?"

I took my hand off my hippo and stared at Teresa. "All of *who?*"

"There's Jessa, of course. But it's Tim and Lydia too. It's pretty obvious that they wish you and Jessa were the couple. That way, you could all double date and have movie night and go to fucking brunch, like I know Lydia is dying to do."

"Jesus, Teresa. What you're saying . . . it's starting to sound crazy. Is it the drugs? Are they making you paranoid?"

That hit a nerve. With a snarl, Teresa stormed my way and grabbed my chin, forcing eye contact. "Sometimes you're so superior, Lawson. Sometimes you're so fucking superior I can't stand you." She kicked over the game set between me and Parker, sending marbles flying every which way.

The marbles went rolling and skidding across the hardwood until there was just one last marble, rolling noisily over the uneven floor. While it meandered on, searching for its elusive resting place, I glanced around the room. Dylan was cowering in the corner. Parker's hands were raised defensively. Jimmy and his girl were frozen, the bottle of Jim Beam between them, mid-pass.

There was no way to recover from the scene Teresa and I had just made. The party was over. Unsalvageable. I wasn't sure about my relationship with Teresa. I thought we'd progressed past her jealousy. I'd believed our troubles were behind us. Clearly, that wasn't so.

It was up to me to decide what happened next. If Teresa and I parted ways. Or if I took the drastic measure I knew I'd have to take to give our relationship a fighting chance.

I got up, dusted off my jeans, and extended a hand to Teresa.

She eyed me uncertainly. Still—she placed her hand in mine.

"Let's go," I said, "up to the roof."

"Okay," she whispered, "What about . . ." Her eyes moved right, toward her friends, then snapped back to mine.

"Stay as long as you like," I said, addressing everyone in the room at once. "Dylan knows how to lock up."

I led Teresa out of the apartment, and up the stairs, all the way to the roof. The stars (as usual) were invisible in the Hollywood sky, but all the lights on the hills glittered in their place. There was a bite to the breeze, so I handed my hoodie to Teresa. She wrapped it around her shoulders, then lowered herself onto the nearest chaise lounge.

"Let me tell you," I said slowly, "what I'm going to do."

She fixed her dark, liquid eyes on me. "All right."

"I have to finish the record," I began.

"I know that . . ."

I put up a hand. "Let me speak. *I have to finish the record*. But, after that, I won't see Jessa anymore. Not as a friend, not as a client. I won't speak to her for any reason."

Teresa stared out at the twinkling hills. "I think," she said, "that's best."

I closed my eyes and let the cool breeze move over my eyelids.

What was necessary would not be easy. I didn't have a lot of close friends, and after all Jessa and I had been through, our friendship felt like something earned. Something deserved. Jessa was also a client and my main connection to Charlie Jackson. Cutting contact with her would be a blow to the studio and, by extension, my career.

It felt like too much to ask. It felt like too much to lose. But I knew that if there was going to be any chance for me and Teresa, it simply had to be.

Chapter 23

The morning after Christmas, all I wanted was to be alone with my new guitar. In the early hours, Tim and Lydia had taken off for the greater Tucson area to see Tim's rootin'-tootin', gun-shootin' family. That meant the studio was all mine.

When I slipped out of bed and removed my new guitar from the coat closet, I was careful not to wake Teresa. Things had turned pretty heavy the night before, and I figured we could both use some breathing room.

In the studio, there was no sign of the previous evening's festivities. Obviously, Tim and his buddies had stayed up doing the old scrub-down. It was also creepy-quiet. Fleetingly, I thought about the pistol that Tim kept in the closet, in a box behind the condenser mics. Too bad I had no idea how to use a gun. If some armed intruder decided to rip Tim off while I was in the studio, I wouldn't be able to do a damn thing about it.

I shook off that rather grim thought and filled Gargamel's bowl—I, of course, had been charged with feline feeding duties. Then I got comfy in one of Tim's desk chairs and opened up my new guitar case for only the second time in my life. I figured that guitar couldn't be as perfect as I remembered. But then, there it was. That shining acoustic, all dramatic curves and mother-of-pearl inlay. Of course, the real magic was in its sound. The deep, honeyed tones bounced around the plaster walls, filling the room. I paused, letting the vibrations pass through me until I shivered.

After that, I just *played*. Anything and everything that

came into my head. Songs I'd written with Jessa. Songs I'd learned when I was a kid. Songs I'd never attempted, but was able to figure out from memory. I didn't put down my guitar until late afternoon—and that was only because I had a sudden urge to listen to the record all the way through. I wanted to figure out which sections would benefit most from my new guitar's distinctive tone.

With a rush of energy, I pulled up the record on Tim's computer and played the whole thing, start to finish. It wasn't hard to choose the parts I wanted to re-record. They jumped out at me immediately. It was amazing how closely the parts I had indicated matched the parts Charlie thought needed "something." I hadn't come up to the studio with the intention of recording, but I was inspired by my discovery.

Like a man on a mission, I searched the top of the closet where Tim stored all his best mics and located the studio condenser that had always served me best. I set it up, tested it, and got down to the business of recording. When I was satisfied with my performances, I made adjustments until the new tracks blended in with the mix. Before I knew it, the sky was dark, and I was finished.

My plan was to email Jessa a link to our songs. If she approved of the work I'd done, she could pass on the link to Charlie. At another time, and in another life, I would have hopped on the train, rode into North Hollywood, and delivered the music to Jessa in person. But things had changed for me. I had to think before I acted. I had to anticipate how Teresa would feel about any move I made. It felt a little bit like living in a straitjacket, but everybody has to make sacrifices sometimes.

My time, I guess, had come.

~ ~ ~

When Jessa called the following morning, I was ready. I grabbed my phone after half a ring so it wouldn't wake

Teresa, who was still sleeping off another night out. Then I stepped out into the hall. "What do you think?"

"I love it," Jessa breathed. "I mean, this is it, Law."

"Are you sure?" I asked, mostly just because I wanted to hear her say it again.

"Yes! I couldn't ask for anything more. You already know how I felt about the last version of the record. You made our songs sound like something off the radio. But those new guitar tracks—they make all the difference. I always think you've impressed me as much as I could be impressed. Then there's something more."

I blushed with the compliment. "Then I guess we've got our record," I said. "Can you forward the link to Charlie?"

"Oh." Jessa paused. "Charlie's already listened to it."

"Really?"

"Yes. I mean . . . he's here. We listened together."

"Okay. Great. What did he think?"

"He thinks it's perfect too. But wait," she said, "hold on." For a few seconds, the receiver crackled in my ear. Then Jessa was back on the line. "Charlie wants to know if you can save the files to a few flash drives. By New Year's Eve."

"Sure. Simple enough. But what's happening on New Year's Eve?"

"Well, Law, Charlie wants to bring some demos to a party one of those big-shot friends of his is throwing." Jessa was playing it cool, but I could hear the excitement buzzing in her voice. "He wants to show off his pet project . . . and, you know . . . see if any interesting opportunities present themselves."

"You have no idea how pleased Tim will be to know that." Charlie had never admitted any specific plans to try to make back his investment, but it was starting to sound like he had something up his sleeve.

"Of course Charlie wants to bring us too," Jessa added. "Can you clear your schedule?"

I hesitated. "I'm not sure. I think I should be with Teresa on New Year's." Last New Year's Eve, Teresa had gone off with her friends, and I'd spent the night in the studio with a band. At the time, it was no big deal. But, lately, Teresa and I had been a little off. No matter what we did, the wrong notes kept sounding between us.

"Bring her!" Jessa suggested amiably. "Tell her there will be free food. Drinks. Everything. Charlie's friends do not disappoint in that regard."

I had to decline. "I'm sorry. I'll have the demos ready, but I won't be able to be there. Not this time." I wished we could all go out to Charlie's party together. That Teresa, Jessa, Charlie, and I could be one merry crew. But I knew that was impossible.

Jessa didn't press the issue. I figured she knew what I knew. That, as the singer, she was the face of our musical partnership. Her presence was far more important than mine.

After I hung up, Teresa dragged herself out of the bedroom. I hadn't realized she was listening in, but I didn't mind. "Won't be where?" she asked, rubbing eyes still puffy from sleep.

"Charlie wants me to go to a party with him on New Year's Eve to pass out demos. I said I couldn't make it."

"Why not?"

"I want to spend New Year's with you."

Teresa fidgeted. "Are you sure, Lawson? I know how you feel about clubs, and New Year's Eve is the biggest club night of the year. Anyway . . . won't Tim want you to network?"

Teresa didn't say any more, but I could practically see her thoughts written in the air between us. She didn't want me tagging along with her. I was going to cramp her style. Harsh her mellow. I was a walking buzzkill. It reminded me of something my mother had said once. *It's like pulling teeth, trying to get you to have any fun.*

"Right," I said, pretending not to be insulted, "I guess we've both got some pretty important obligations."

"Yes," Teresa said, pretending not to be incredibly relieved, "I guess we do."

Chapter 24

Our New Year's Eve host was a slight man in a tux, who Charlie assured us had produced several of the latest blockbuster movies. His house was built on a sheer cliff. The structure snaked along the edge, deferring to boulders and ledges. Its whole south face was made of glass.

While Charlie shot the breeze with a few buddies, Jessa and I gazed out over Los Angeles and its adjacent municipalities. An indigo sky melted to electric orange over the shapes of so many familiar structures. The massive US Bank skyscraper that lorded over downtown. The Franklin Hotel. The Capitol Records building, with its space-age silhouette.

Jessa reached a hand toward the window glass. "Did you ever think we'd be in a place like this? Or see anything like what we're looking at now?" she asked. "I mean, when we were back in Gunther."

I shook my head. "Never. I couldn't even have imagined it."

But we didn't have much time to spend admiring the view. It was time for show and tell, and Jessa and I were the objects of interest. As the party progressed, Charlie moved easily from person to person, group to group, always with the two of us in tow. He had the flash drives I made in an inside pocket of his blazer, but gave out very few. Most of the time, he just boasted over our music while I stared at my shoes and Jessa sipped her champagne.

During a brief interlude at the requisite *hors d'oeuvres*

table, Jessa grabbed onto Charlie's arm. "Charlie, are we doing enough? Are we *saying* enough?" she demanded.

He chuckled. "Jessa. I assure you. No one wants to deal with a couple of jaded Hollywood fast-talkers. You're refreshing—the pretty girl and the hometown kid. My friends are loving you. I promise."

Charlie always appeared so relaxed, like he was just palling around with his friends. But all the time he was keeping close tabs on the impression we were making. I was glad to know it was a good one.

~ ~ ~

For most of the night the party could be accurately termed a low-key affair, but as midnight approached the atmosphere shifted. Shrill, reckless laughter echoed through the room as intoxicated guests shrieked and chased each other.

I worked hard to keep close to Jessa and Charlie in the chaos, but after a caterer passed me a bubbling flute of champagne, I found myself surrounded by strangers. Jessa and Charlie, who had been right at my elbow, were nowhere to be seen. It was nearly midnight, so I shrugged and raised my champagne glass high.

Seconds later, a sloppy, booming countdown rocked the room. The noise level rose to ear-murdering decibels. Paper horns were blown. Feet were stamped. I turned around, and around, watching the celebration unfold. To my surprise, I locked eyes with Jessa, who was twenty feet across the room. She smiled and mouthed "Happy New Year," then stepped in my direction, champagne glass raised, arm outstretched.

I immediately began pushing toward her, revelers in my path be damned.

When I was halfway there, Charlie moved into my line of vision. He wrapped his arm around Jessa and eased her in for a slow dance.

She broke eye contact with me as Charlie dipped her, sending her momentarily out of view. When she reappeared, they were laughing. And then, they were kissing.

I stopped dead, overcome by the sensation that someone had heaved a brick directly into my gut.

I looked away. What Jessa and Charlie did with their lips wasn't any of my business. I couldn't fully explain my nausea. I guess it was just that it was so unexpected. Charlie was obviously in love with Jessa, but she'd never indicated any interest in him.

Before I could really process what I'd just seen, an old lady in a blue cocktail dress and eye makeup smeared to her eyebrows yanked me in for a slobbery kiss. I closed my eyes against the assault on my senses, struggling not to breathe in her nostril-tingling perfume or feel her pruned smoker's lips grating against my skin.

I could hear her old lady friends cackling at her boldness.

~ ~ ~

After I pried myself away from my aged assailant, I wandered, lost, through the room. Long after the stroke of midnight, partygoers continued toasting, clinking their champagne flutes together clumsily. Someone was singing "Auld Lang Syne" in a slurry baritone. I staggered aimlessly through the chaos until somebody gave a solid yank on my hood.

When I turned around, there was Jessa, stifling a giggle. "Oh my goodness, Lawson!" She dunked her finger into her champagne and rubbed it against my cheek. "You have lipstick all over your face. In a most unearthly shade of pink, no less! You better let me clean you up or you might be in some trouble when you get home, my dear."

"If the lipstick's owner is over a hundred, I don't think it counts," I said with a weak laugh. "Maybe your midnight kiss was more rewarding?" I did my best to sound lighthearted. So Jessa wouldn't think I was judging her.

Still, she blushed intensely and cast her gaze to the floor. "You saw? Of course you saw. I guess I should have told you, Lawson. Charlie and I are seeing each other. Sort of." She tossed her hair and looked at everything in the room besides me. "It's not exactly defined. Early stages stuff, you know."

"Yeah. Sure. I know how it is."

For some reason, neither of us could come up with anything to say after that. We stood in silence until Charlie came tromping through the crowd. He stepped between me and Jessa, throwing an arm around each of us. "Ready to go?" he asked.

"Very," Jessa said. She seemed winded.

"Great. Me too," Charlie replied. "My trainer's coming at five."

At first, I was surprised. I expected Charlie to stay up all night, mainlining coke in one of the hot tubs built into the rocks outside. He fit the mold of a Hollywood cliché, with his back slapping and his expert schmoozing. But, when I really thought about it, I knew Charlie was no party boy. He had to be disciplined to stay in the kind of shape he was in— and, of course, to get a hotshot job like the one he had before the age of forty. It didn't take a brainiac to figure that out.

~ ~ ~

On our winding way out of the Hollywood Hills, Charlie glanced at me in the rearview. "I'll have to drop you at Jessa's place, Lawson. As I'm sure you know, we won't get near Hollywood Boulevard on New Year's Eve."

I didn't know. Or at least I hadn't thought much about it. Once again, I was surprised. Considering Charlie and Jessa were a hot new item, I figured he'd want to ditch me as soon as humanly possible. You know, so he could whisk Jessa up to his slick Westwood condo and put on the moves.

Not so. After a speedy jaunt up the 170, Charlie turned north on Lankershim and made an abrupt stop in front of Jessa's building. He got out of the car just long enough to give her an oddly shy kiss goodbye. And then, after a wave to both of us, he was back behind the wheel.

As Charlie peeled away, Jessa's heels clicked on the pavement as she joined me on the sidewalk. While crickets chirped their shrill music, we watched his luxury automobile disappear into the night.

"So Charlie's not staying over," I said.

"Lawson!" Jessa punched me in the arm with playful fury. "Charlie and I just started seeing each other. We're not there yet. Or anywhere near it." Then she took my elbow and we headed down the path to her generic North Hollywood apartment.

I'd never been inside Jessa's place at night. It had the same paint-and-cleaner smell it did during the day, but I could also catch the scent of jasmine floating in through the screens. And without harsh sunbeams illuminating the synthetic countertops and cheap, too-white kitchen tile, the place actually felt cozy.

"You want anything?" Jessa asked as she loaded a few dishes into the dishwasher. "Water? A glass of milk? *Pancakes?*"

I glanced at the clock on the microwave. "I should probably get going. I'm not sure how late the trains run tonight."

"You're really going to try to make it back to Hollywood tonight? Is Teresa expecting you?"

"Well, no," I admitted. "She'll be out till morning. She went dancing with her friends."

"Then, stay! I have a couch with your name all over it."

I didn't want to tell Jessa the kinds of accusations that would fly my way if I played slumber party. But then, Teresa didn't have to know. "I guess that would be okay," I said at last.

"I've got a few extra blankets you can use. A pillow too, if you're lucky." Jessa disappeared into her room and, a few moments later, emerged with an armful of bedding. "Here you go." She dumped the whole lot of them on the sofa.

I nodded. "Thanks."

While Jessa rounded up some shoes and dresses that hadn't made the cut for her evening ensemble, I spread out the blankets on the couch and sat down heavily. In that moment, I had the urge to tell her that things weren't quite right with me. That I needed to talk to somebody. Or maybe just sit with me until I went to sleep. But of course it was only the champagne messing with my head. I'd only had a few gulps, but they'd tasted rancid.

So all I said was "Happy New Year," and "goodnight." And then I stretched out on Jessa's generic beige sofa and passed out cold.

Chapter 25

On New Year's Day, I woke to one of those perfect California mornings. The sun was bright, the birds were twittering, and the champagne-induced melancholy that had seized me the night before was long gone.

With what I can only describe as good cheer, I folded my blankets neatly into a pile. I wanted to say goodbye to Jessa, but when I peered into the open door of her room, she was snoring into her comforter and looking about as asleep as a person could be. I decided a note would have to do, so I penned one on an old receipt and headed out into the North Hollywood haze to catch the train.

The trip was, as usual, short and sweet. The metro rolled past Universal Studios and pulled up to the station under the Kodak Center with its usual screech. I hopped out onto the tile and hurried up the stairs, my footsteps echoing through the empty station.

Out on the Boulevard, I stepped quickly through the trash and the tinsel. For the first time in weeks, I couldn't wait to get home. I guess it took a night spent elsewhere to really miss my apartment—and Teresa. Things between us had been tense, but I was eager to move past all that. To move forward.

The gate in front of my building was cool and pleasant to the touch. I liked how heavy and substantial it felt in my hand. The bright sunlight warmed my back, then fell away as I passed through the cave-like hallway. Finally, I was in front of #4. I unlocked the door and got ready to take in all my precious, familiar things: the faux-suede sectional, the records arranged artfully on the wall, the well-worn dining set.

But when I pushed open the door and raised my head, my smile evaporated. The apartment I saw was not the one I left. Not even close. The coffee table and the couch cushions were askew. Jagged pieces of wood, crumpled paper, and other debris were strewn everywhere. I blinked, and then blinked again. Nothing changed.

All I could think was that some burglar had ransacked the place. Immediately, I thought of Teresa. Was she at home when the intruders showed up? If so, she would have had no way to defend herself. Unlike Tim, I didn't have a single weapon in the house. Not even a really sharp knife. Not even a can of pepper spray.

My eyes shot to the bedroom door, which was firmly closed. I couldn't help but imagine the worst. Stricken, I lurched forward and grabbed the doorknob. And turned. And then . . . I stopped.

I swiveled my neck, and scanned the room once more. Teresa's tablet was sitting pretty on the coffee table, and her spanking new record player was still plugged into the opposite wall.

I forced my eyes to focus on the detritus that was scattered everywhere. Most of it was made of wood, some in large chunks, some in tiny fragments. In a way, it was all too familiar. Then I saw the strings. When I picked up a tiny, broken piece of mother-of-pearl, I sank slowly to my knees.

My home had not been robbed. But my most treasured possession in the world had been destroyed. Very thoroughly—and deliberately—it appeared. I almost couldn't fathom an action so senseless, or so cruel. I also couldn't imagine who could have done such a thing. But I needed to know. And fast. Teresa had clearly brought the party home the night before. She was going to have to tell me which of her druggie friends had smashed my guitar.

Hot tears burned the whites of my eyes as I struggled to my feet, then threw open the bedroom door. Inside, Teresa and Dylan were sprawled out on the bed, sound asleep. They lay across one another, by all appearances exhausted and happy. As if they'd had a wonderful night and pleasant dreams.

"Teresa," I croaked.

She stirred, then rolled over and mumbled into the sheets. "I'm tired, Lawson."

"I know." I grabbed her wrist. "But I need you to wake up. My guitar—it's been destroyed."

Very slowly, Teresa raised herself and leaned back against the headboard. "What are you talking about?"

"My guitar," I repeated. "It's been smashed to pieces."

"Oh. That's . . . I mean, that's terrible." For some reason, she glanced at Dylan. He looked away.

"It probably happened after you went to bed. Still, I need you to tell me who could have done it."

Teresa frowned. "I don't know."

"Well, who was here last night? Tell me. Please," I begged.

"Let's see. Who was here? Jimmy. It could have been him. Dylan, don't you think it must have been Jimmy?"

"Sure," he said, rubbing his face. He reached for his glasses, which were perched on the windowsill. "Could have been Jimmy."

That was a start. "Well, Jesus. I always thought Jimmy was a nice kid. What was he on?" I shook my head. "Never mind. How do I get a hold of him?"

Nice kid or not, Jimmy wasn't off the hook. No way. He was going to have to scrimp and save until he bought me a new guitar just like the one he ruined. Not that any other guitar would be the same. I really wanted *my* guitar. The one

Jessa had picked out and played in the store and tested until she knew it was perfect. The one I'd opened up slowly in Tim's apartment and touched with reverence. The one I'd used on the record.

"I don't know how to reach Jimmy right now," Teresa claimed.

"How can you not know? He lives with Dylan."

Teresa's eyes shot in Dylan's direction again, but he was busy trying to blend into the sheets. "Jimmy moved out weeks ago. He couldn't pay rent. I don't think he has a permanent place. He's . . . he's been crashing on couches."

I didn't believe her. "Jimmy did a cruel thing. Why are you protecting him?"

"I'm not."

"Then stop lying to me!"

Teresa suddenly burst into tears. "Are you dense, Lawson? Jimmy didn't do anything."

"What do you mean?"

"I did it, Lawson! Get it now?"

While Teresa sobbed, I just stood there, struck dumb, waiting for my brain to catch up with the stupid, idiot world. When it did, I was nauseous. "Why would you do something like that to me? How *could* you do something like that to me?"

Teresa trembled. "Well, fuck! We were out, and it was crazy, and we were all having the best time. Dylan was really happy because Parker was practically superglued to his side all night. Then midnight came along, and that hardbody bartender from Epitome showed up and, out of nowhere, Parker *left* with him. So we came back here and Dylan got all weepy. He just started burning letters from Parker he'd been carrying around in his pocket since forever. It made him feel so much better. It was like a high!" Teresa wiped at her eyes. "After that, we just . . . got carried away."

I was mystified. "What the hell does any of that have to do with me, or my guitar?"

Teresa balled up her fists. "You're hurting me, just like Parker hurts Dylan. Do you really think everything is fine with us? With me? I hate her!"

"I guess you're talking about Jessa."

"Of course I'm talking about Jessa, Lawson! I'm sick of her strutting around with her boobs and her hips stuffed into a dress two sizes too small. Posing all over the place like she's some femme fatale, when she's just a small-town girl with fifteen extra pounds on her and hair full of split ends. You say you won't see her when the record's finished, but I know I'll never be rid of her. She'll always think of some new reason to be near you."

I gaped. "Teresa. You're so wrong. You're so wrong about everything. Jessa's with *Charlie*."

"It doesn't matter with her! Maybe she doesn't want one, when she can have two. She got to have both of you on New Year's Eve, didn't she? The rich fuck on one arm, and her boy toy on the other."

I cringed. I'd heard that last phrase before. "Teresa, why didn't you just ask me not to go? If you were still upset, why didn't you just talk to me?"

"You never talk to me anymore," she whined.

I pressed against the doorframe, trying to get my thoughts straight—but no dice. I almost for one second felt guilty, because maybe I shouldn't have locked myself up in the studio all week. Just maybe I should have said "fuck it" to promoting the record and stuck with Teresa on New Year's Eve, no matter what she said to me. But then I remembered my guitar—once perfect, now broken and destroyed.

My bones shook inside my skin. "I'm leaving."

"All right," Teresa said in a little mosquito-sized voice.

Dylan clung to the sheets.

I almost felt bad for him. For being caught up in the crossfire. Then I remembered he'd been there with Teresa all night. Knowing him, he'd cheered her on.

Out in the living room, I rooted through Teresa's purse until I found her car keys. Then I headed out of the apartment, down the hall, and into the lot where Teresa's mud-brown Crown Victoria was parked. I hopped in, fired the thing up, and got on the freeway going west. I didn't shoot for anyplace in particular. I just aimed myself toward the sea, and when there was no more street to speak of, I nosed into the first spot I could find along the curb.

On the beach, I laid down somewhere between the boardwalk and the water and let the sand envelop me and the sea air ease my hurt. For hours, I listened to the water breaking on the beach, while a bunch of nuisance seagulls fought over French fries on the boardwalk. The whole time, I expected a lot of feelings to wash over me, to overwhelm me, but they didn't. I just felt sort of empty.

It was nearly dusk when I finally got up and brushed the sand off my jeans. I thought I might just stay on the coast all night long, and sleep rough. Until I remembered a story John had told me. A couple he knew in high school had tried spending the night on the beach. Everything was peace and magic until a homeless guy knocked them both in the head with a shovel.

With that unsettling thought in my mind, I located Teresa's car and drove my ass home.

~ ~ ~

Back in Hollywood, I braced myself before entering my apartment. I wasn't sure I could stand seeing the tiniest splinter of my ruined guitar. But when I let myself inside, I found no trace of my guitar, or Teresa, and the living room was tidier than I had seen it for weeks.

I climbed into bed and burrowed under the covers, but I couldn't sleep. I was still wide awake when Teresa came home at five, but I didn't let on. When she shook my shoulder and called my name, I just sighed and rolled over.

Chapter 26

When Jessa called me two days after the New Year, her voice was like a brass band playing directly into my ear.

"Lawson! Good news!" she practically shouted. "Going to that awful party may have paid off after all."

"Oh yeah?" Already, I regretted picking up the phone. Talking to Jessa made me feel strange and disconnected. She had no idea what was going on in my world. She had no clue what had happened since I'd crashed on her couch. It was like she was calling from some other dimension.

"Charlie says one of his friends might have a gig for us. Something big."

"A gig?" I was immediately disappointed. When I'd gone to that party, I was hoping one of Charlie's industry friends might consider using a track in a film or on television. That would be a big deal for the studio.

"Yes, a gig," Jessa confirmed. "I don't have anything more. Charlie won't give me details until he knows we're ready to get onstage."

"Are we even a band?" I asked crankily.

Jessa was all soothing words. "Oh, Lawson," she drawled. "I know this is sudden, and we haven't even had a minute to discuss it. But let's at least find out what Charlie's got. All he wants to do is listen to us play a few songs. You know . . . just to make sure we're tight."

"We're tight."

"I know that. So let's go in there and prove it."

I sighed. I had minimal interest in Charlie's "gig." But it wasn't like it would take any effort to puke out those songs for old Charlie. I knew them so well I could play them without thinking. I could play them half asleep. I could play them half dead.

So I got up, yanked on a pair of jeans, and slid my old guitar out from under the bed. Teresa, of course, wouldn't want me at Jessa's place or anywhere near it. But Teresa was not at home, and I had no further plans to inform her of my activities. If she wanted to know what I was up to, well . . . she'd have to get off her ass and stalk me.

With that thought, I hefted my body out the door and transported it, via train, to Jessa's apartment. As soon as I got there, I wished I would have stayed at home. The whole mood was off. Charlie was striding through the room and making big hand gestures as if he were *presiding*. Jessa was huddled on the couch, nervous as a schoolgirl.

I let myself zone out. Charlie's voice became a drone. I almost nodded off. Then Jessa's elbow landed deep in my rib cage, and I sat up with a start. "First track!" she hissed. "Now."

I played but I couldn't enjoy it. Charlie's eyes were locked on Jessa the whole time, and she knew it. She was playing to him like he was an audience. Trying too hard. Overacting. Charlie was eating it up.

"I'm pleasantly surprised," he exclaimed the moment we were finished. "You two fall right in together."

I rolled my eyes. Jessa and I had played those songs together hundreds of times.

Charlie uncrossed his ankles and leaned toward Jessa with a big smile slapped on his face. I could see practically every one of his pearly whites—and, boy, were those things pearly.

"Jessa. You're more of a front woman than I realized," he said. "Still, you got a little sloppy on your transitions when you were interacting with me."

"Oh. Well, I'll work on that, Charlie," Jessa said seriously. As if she had just received counsel from someone very wise.

Then Charlie turned to me. "Lawson. I have to say. You're dead on. The only thing is . . . something's not quite right." He drummed his fingers on the coffee table.

"Something like what?"

"I don't know how to put it, but it's like you're not playing the guitar like a guitar. You don't, you know, pick it up and show it who's boss." He leapt to his feet and demonstrated a rock stance.

I bristled. "Am I laying back on the beat?"

"You're not, no. I guess it's more a matter of style."

Jessa cleared her throat. "I think Lawson's style is just fine. Remember, Charlie. We're not a rock band."

Charlie paused, as if considering Jessa's words. Then he sat back down. "You know what? You're right. You're something else altogether, thanks to those beats. I guess the real question is whether you'll be able to reproduce those live, Lawson."

"Sure." I shrugged. "I'll probably need some new equipment."

"Well, let me know how much that will cost. I'll write you a check."

"I don't need a sponsor, Charlie. I have the cash."

He frowned. "Of course not. That wasn't what I meant."

Jessa smiled a little too brightly. "I think we all know what we have to do. Why don't we call it a day?" I could tell she wanted to head off the argument that was brewing in the air. "Lawson and I can meet up tomorrow. I'll practice tonight, and he'll make sure my transitions are coming along."

"Sounds good," Charlie said. "Let me know how that goes."

"Can I come by your place around noon tomorrow, Lawson?" Jessa touched my knee. "*Lawson*. Are you listening?"

"Yes. Noon. Fine," I muttered.

Jessa made a face. Clearly, my lack of enthusiasm displeased her. But, the fact was, I'd already begun to wonder if this gig was for real—or just some bullshit Charlie had cooked up to get in Jessa's good graces. And/or her pants.

I put my guitar away at warp speed. All I wanted was to get out of there. Jessa and I had put on our little show. And Charlie had put on his. And it was time for me to go.

~ ~ ~

On the train ride home, I seethed. Jessa was a smart girl. I couldn't understand why she didn't see what a big act Charlie was putting on. Like he was a band manager or some hip A&R guy for a record company instead of a glorified salesman.

While the train rolled along I tried to imagine myself confronting Charlie. Delivering a series of insults, dousing them with sarcasm, and setting everything on fire with a final cutting remark. Then I tried to think of something I could say to Charlie that would make him so angry he would hit me. Because then I could hit him back, and no one could blame me or say it was my fault. Charlie would wipe me on the concrete—obviously—but it would be worth it. If I could get in just one good swing.

At first I was really enjoying my angry little fantasies. Then, somewhere around Universal Studios, an unavoidable question forced itself into my mind: *Why was I so angry at Charlie?* He could be pushy, but he'd always treated me decently. He was in love with Jessa, and it would have been easy for Charlie to ignore me or exclude me. He never did.

As the train rattled on toward Hollywood, I kept on puzzling. Finally, I had to consider whether maybe, on some level, I was jealous of Charlie. The idea wasn't entirely nuts. After all, Charlie had done very well for himself. He had a hotshot job, a condo in Westwood, and a couple of rental properties. Still, when I really thought about it, I knew I didn't care about any of those things. I wanted to be a success, sure, but as an audio engineer. I wanted to build on my craft and engineer albums that I could be proud of.

The realization was not comforting. Because if I didn't envy Charlie's accomplishments, then there was only one potential source for my jealousy. And that was his budding relationship with Jessa Warlow. It seemed impossible that some part of me might still have feelings for Jessa, without the rest of me knowing it. But I had to admit. My Charlie allergy had appeared pretty quickly after I caught that eyeful of Charlie and Jessa swapping spit.

Suddenly, I was sweating. I hoped like hell that I wasn't still in love with Jessa Warlow. I'd fallen for her back in Gunther, when I was just a kid. When I didn't know any better. I knew I'd be a fool to do it again. Worse, what kind of guy would that make me if I did? If all those times I'd called Teresa paranoid, or crazy . . . she was right?

The thought was too much for me. I turned toward the window and stared at the tile walls of the tunnel until they blurred. I just wanted to get home, race up to the studio, and get lost in my work. So I didn't have to think anything at all.

Chapter 27

The next day I woke up, rolled over, and grabbed for my phone, which I'd propped up on the windowsill. I swiped the screen and checked the time—it was quarter to noon. I didn't usually sleep in so late, but I'd spent a long, grueling night mixing for some teenagers in Boyle Heights who did rock *en español*—and did it well.

As I headed for the kitchen to brew some coffee to sip leisurely on the roof of my building, I remembered Jessa had invited herself over. That she would be at my door any minute. That it was too late to cancel because Jessa would already be riding the train toward Hollywood, guitar case between her knees.

I didn't want to see Jessa. Not after the things that had occurred to me on that very same train. I tried to convince myself that my sudden distaste for Charlie was nothing more than the result of a bad mood. Besides, there was no denying that Charlie had been a lot pushier ever since he got a demo in his hands and decided it was time to play band manager. That, I decided, would be enough to get under anybody's skin.

When Jessa breezed in twenty minutes later, she gave me a once-over. "You're wearing the same clothes."

"I worked all night," I told her stiffly.

She nodded toward my guitar. "Where's the new one? I meant to ask you yesterday."

"I don't want to talk about it."

Jessa shrugged. She wasn't one to press me for answers. She didn't have the patience. "Just listen, I guess." Jessa made herself comfortable on the end of the sectional and took out her guitar. "I practiced all the changes last night."

I didn't even know how to explain to her how little I cared about Charlie's uninformed corrections, so I didn't try. I just dragged over a chair from the kitchen table, sat down, and crossed my arms over my chest.

I tried to keep my eyes locked on the ceiling, but eventually my eyes drifted down to Jessa, who was strumming and singing like her life depended on it. My head was suddenly full of questions.

I told Teresa I couldn't think of Jessa "that way"—not anymore—but was that really true? Or was it just what I wanted so badly to believe? As much as I didn't want to know, I *had* to know.

For the first time since Jessa had moved to Los Angeles, I forced myself to really look at her. What did I see? Full lips and feline eyes. A cotton dress taut against her curves. Beauty I couldn't deny. The honest truth was that, no, I wasn't immune to Jessa's charms. But that didn't mean I was in love with her either.

I guess I was staring because Jessa stopped playing her guitar. "Are you even listening?"

I didn't answer. I was feeling very strange. Light-headed. I scooted my chair closer to Jessa's.

"Why are you looking at me like that?" she asked.

Again, I didn't answer. At least not with words. I figured I could either sit around all day, analyzing, and debating. Or I could do what, all of a sudden, I knew I had to do. Very gently, I leaned in. And kissed Jessa on the lips.

She made a small sound of surprise and dismay. Then she kissed me back.

A surge of heat pulsed through my body. But I still felt no rush of emotion, no tug at my heart. If anything, there was a conspicuous kind of emptiness. Satisfied with the results, I pulled away.

"Why did you do that?" Jessa asked breathlessly. Her eyes, large and curious, peered into mine.

I shrugged. "I just wanted to see how it felt."

She paused. "Okay. How did it feel?"

"Nothing like it used to." Truer words had never been spoken. I wasn't in love with Jessa. And, boy, was I glad to know that for sure. Almost triumphantly, I moved to kiss her again.

Jessa held up her guitar. "Then why are you still doing that?"

It was a good question. I didn't have a clear answer. I guess I was possessed by an impulse. I was simply doing exactly what I felt like doing, in that moment. Like other people did all the time. No matter who it hurt, or who got in the way.

When Jessa loosened her grip on her guitar, I plucked it out of her arms and leaned it against the coffee table. The rest of the afternoon, starting with that second, stretched out in front of me like a mystery. I didn't know what I was going to do. How far I'd go. What Jessa would allow. That made me feel more alive, more awake, than I'd felt in days. Maybe even weeks.

I moved toward Jessa, but it was her turn to surprise me. When I covered her mouth with mine, she met me with big, gasping sighs like a drowning person sucking air. Instead of pushing me away, she twisted my T-shirt in a death grip, pulling my body down against hers.

The intensity of her reaction was a complete shock to me. With what I can only describe as revulsion, I leapt to my feet. The heat that burned me from the inside out left as quickly as it came. I felt very cold.

While Jessa tried to catch her breath, I went to the window. The sky outside was white with pale winter sunshine. I stared into it, trying to go blind. Even when I sensed Jessa behind me, I didn't turn around. I kept on staring directly into the sun, my fists balled up so tightly they cramped.

When Jessa put a hand on my shoulder, I shook it away. "Please tell me what just happened, Lawson," she whispered.

I didn't think I could make myself speak, but then there were the words. "You're with Charlie," I said, "but you want me. I mean, you're practically dying to screw around on him, aren't you?"

I could just make out Jessa's startled expression reflected in the window glass.

"You're not even really into Charlie, are you? All you like is what he can do for your music career. I guess now that you're in L.A. you think you can have me on the side again."

"Law, no. You don't understand."

"You're already fucking him, too."

"*Who?*"

I whirled around. "Charlie! When you called me to tell me what you thought about the first draft of our record, he was there. Obviously, he stayed the night. Then on New Year's, you played it off like everything between you was innocent."

"Lawson, please. You just give me the word and Charlie's gone. Just give me the word . . . and I'm all yours."

"So you think I'd break up with Teresa to be with you. On a dime."

"I didn't say that."

"You didn't have to. I know you. You think you're irresistible. Your ego is unbelievable."

Jessa sputtered. "Lawson, you kissed *me*. I never wanted to get in the middle of your relationship. If you said those things to me back in Gunther, I'd have said you were right. But not this time. This time you're not being fair."

I didn't want to hear any more. Jessa could twist and bend reality all she wanted to, but I wasn't going to stand there and listen. I was just about to throw her out, but before I could move a muscle, the front door flew open.

When I glanced up, there was Teresa, standing frozen. Her purple sunglasses slipped down her nose. "What is this?"

"Rehearsal," I said weakly. "Charlie's orders."

"Right," Teresa intoned. There was acid in her voice.

"I was just leaving," Jessa added.

"Good." Teresa's eyes bored holes through Jessa as she hustled to pack up her guitar. "You're not welcome here. Lawson knows that."

Jessa looked at me with a mixture of surprise and confusion. Then she grabbed her guitar, put her head down, and marched straight out of the apartment.

Teresa slammed the door behind her.

I slunk to the couch.

After a few tense seconds, Teresa flopped down beside me.

While I sat there, hands folded tightly under my arms and feet on the coffee table, I tried to feel something. It was weird. I knew I had just become one of the most terrible things anyone could be—a cheater. At the same time, the past half hour felt like something that happened in a dream, or maybe on TV. I half expected to hear canned laugh tracks.

"I don't know what went on here," Teresa said finally. "I don't want to know. But please, Lawson. Can we call it even?"

"Even?"

She nodded.

So Teresa believed I wanted to get caught. That I had plotted some revenge. I was hazy about the reasons behind my actions, but I didn't think Teresa had the right answer. At least not exactly. In fact, as far as I knew, Teresa wasn't due back until much later that afternoon.

"Why aren't you at school?" I asked.

"I dropped my classes," Teresa informed me flatly.

I straightened. "All of them?"

She turned to me, snarling. "Are you really going to get on my case right now, Lawson?"

I shut the fuck up.

Chapter 28

After the disastrous afternoon spent in my living room with Jessa Warlow, my days all ran together. Sleep, record, mix. Mix, record, sleep. Until the morning I woke to find myself drowning. Water filled my nostrils and pooled over my eyes. The sea had swelled and all of Hollywood had flooded. There was no escape. Death, it seemed, was imminent. That was okay by me. It was even sort of a relief. I didn't bother opening my eyes.

As I prepared myself for whatever version of the afterlife awaited me, I heard the low, gruff voice of an old sea captain. "I'm sorry I didn't build you a stronger ship." Then there was a snort. And a snicker.

Without looking, I raised my hand and smacked away the object I could sense right in front of my nose. When I opened my eyes I watched an empty water glass bounce harmlessly against the carpet.

"Matthew Brewer," I said, sitting up. "Why are you in my bedroom?"

He grinned. "Hey, we used to share a bed, remember? I thought you were used to me being all up in your boudoir. But, really, let's not talk about me. What's up with you, kiddo?" He slapped me on the back.

I coughed. "Nothing. I'm ready to take on the world."

"I'm not so sure. You were sleeping like the dead—really, like the *dead*—and it's four o'clock post meridiem, old buddy. You didn't even hear my rather insistent knocking. Teresa had to let me in."

"Right. Well, I edited tracks all last night. That's studio work, for you. That's, you know . . . the nature of the beast." I had taken some more of those sleeping pills my mother used. I needed to get some Z's before I had to be back in the studio. It wasn't my fault they made me sleep a little deeper than usual.

"Ah. I see," Matt said agreeably. As if I didn't know he was humoring me. "I was getting worried. Alli says she hasn't heard from you in ages." Matt glanced in the direction of the living room. "I can't say I feel a lot better now. Your apartment is really depressing, my man. Can't you get your old lady to tidy the place a bit? Maybe not leave her pipes and shit out on the coffee table?"

"I don't care what it looks like around here. I'm thinking about moving anyway," I lied.

"Oh yeah?" Matt perked up. "You should come over to the West Side."

"Maybe I will," I lied again.

"Really glad to hear that, old buddy. I can't even tell you. Now, let's get out of this shithole! I came over here to collect your bones for a mandatory happy hour. No protests permitted."

"I'm not protesting." I rolled out of bed. "Pig 'n' Whistle?"

"Fuck yes. Just like old times."

After I had located a new T-shirt, Matt and I ambled down the Boulevard. We pulled up a couple of stools at the Pig 'n' Whistle's long, wooden bar and, for a couple of hours, it really was just like old times. Still, I sort of wished Matt would stop putting on the pressure. A couple of pitchers in he started talking about how I should really "get my ass west of Fairfax." Then he was cracking jokes about ditching Teresa and finding some collegiate co-eds to keep my bed warm.

"I know you weren't more than moderately in demand in Gunther, Pennsylvania, but these university girls would go crazy for you," he insisted. "They love smart dudes. And a gaunt English major? The janitor would have to bring a mop because . . ."

Matt was still the same old Matt, but I also started to wonder if he thought he was better than me now that he was a college guy and I wasn't.

Matt was keen to make a night of it in Hollywood, but after a final round of foreign lager, I excused myself. I just wasn't having fun anymore.

~ ~ ~

I guess it was my lucky week because not two days later, I was treated to another uninvited guest. While I was putting on a pot of coffee, someone began pounding rather insistently on the front door.

"Teresa, get that!" I yelled. She was in the bedroom, sleeping off yet another hangover. Or whatever it is that happens after you stay up all night doing party drugs with your club friends.

When Teresa failed to respond, I stomped into the living room and threw the door open. Who did I find standing there? *Fucking Charlie.*

"Lawson," he said in a bright, conversational way. As if he always showed up at my place unannounced. "Can I come in?"

I figured Charlie had come by to put on the pressure about that gig he'd been dangling in front of Jessa's nose. I didn't mind letting him know that the performance, and any associated rehearsals, were off. If he demanded to know why, I'd be happy to tell him how Jessa crammed her tongue down my esophagus not ten feet from where he was standing.

When I stepped aside to let Charlie enter, his eyes scanned the room. It was full of half-empty drinks and food wrappers, and even the remains of the cigarettes Teresa had started to let her friends smoke in the house. Charlie pretended not to see. Instead, he dodged the trash and took a seat on the sectional. Then he got down to business.

"Now, Law, this might not be my place. But I came by to find out how you are. Jessa's been worried sick about you."

I almost laughed out loud. "I haven't spoken to Jessa for weeks. What would she know about how I'm doing?"

Charlie cleared his throat. "Well, one of your friends told your sister and your brother that you might be in some kind of trouble. When your sister couldn't reach you, your brother called Jessa. I don't know. Long story. I guess that's how small towns are, right? Word gets around."

So Matt had run his mouth. What a rat he was turning out to be. "Gunther isn't really a small town," I corrected. "It's more like . . . a suburb. Of Philadelphia."

"Right." As if Charlie cared. Either way, Gunther was the sort of non-cosmopolitan municipality he found both quaint and irrelevant. "The point is, I came here to ask you what I can do."

"Charlie, I'm fine. I've been working a lot. That's it."

He wasn't put off so easily. "Come on, Law. We're talking man to man here. Check out this place. Check out *you*. It's obvious you're depressed. Or something. Maybe you're on drugs. I wouldn't know."

"Is that so?" I could hardly believe Charlie's nerve. Rich guys really thought they could say anything to anybody.

"Yeah. It would have to be so. You're at least fifteen pounds lighter than the last time I saw you. You've got circles under your eyes. Your hands shake. All in all, you look like hell. Just like your friend said."

"I've been working through the night. I have deadlines." My voice rose. "Why is that so hard for everyone to understand?"

Charlie put up a hand. "All right. I get the point. At least answer me this. Why won't you talk to Jessa anymore? It's breaking her heart. She adores you, Law. I'd even say she idolizes you in a way—because you're so talented. Why would you cut her out of your life?"

I cringed. I hated the way Charlie was talking to me. Like I was a child or some wayward teen in need of a pep talk. "If Jessa wants answers, she can talk to me herself."

Charlie cast his gaze around the apartment once again. This time he didn't hide his disgust. "Okay. I hear you, Law. I'm not trying to intrude. Just know you can call me anytime you need anything. Or drop by, whenever you want to get out of here for a few hours." He stood and handed me a business card. "Here's all my information. My address is on the back."

I shoved the card in my pocket and opened the door. In the way of a hint.

Charlie stepped out into the dim hallway, lit by the few fluorescent fixtures still in operation. The rest were merely mausoleums for Hollywood's dearly departed moths.

"One more thing," he said. "I'm on my way to LAX right now, but Jessa's house sitting for me. I know she would more than welcome a visit from you."

"House sitting?" Charlie traveled for work all the time. I'd never heard about him needing a house sitter before.

Suddenly, he was fighting a smile. "Well, Jessa's been dying to get out of that horrible North Hollywood apartment. I suggested she try out my place. Not the condo . . . I'm in one of my rental properties in Los Feliz."

"Oh." So Jessa was moving in with the rich bastard. I looked away.

~ ~ ~

After Charlie finally fucked off, I thought I'd be able to breathe easy. You know, really enjoy my apartment's new

Charlie-free status. Instead, I just felt a weird, sickening ache inside of me. Like someone had sucked out all my endorphins with a straw.

While I pinched the bridge of my nose to ward off the monster headache I felt coming on, Teresa tottered out of the bedroom and joined me on the couch. "Was that *Charlie?*" she asked, eager to get the gossip. "What was he talking about?"

"Nothing. Don't worry about it." I stood up and stretched. "All I know is, I need a drink."

Teresa brightened. "I'll get my skateboard, and we'll drink cans of beer in the parking lot like we used to!"

"Sure," I said, "just like we used to." Of course it would be nothing like the way it used to be. But I wanted to drink. Very badly. I wanted to get sloppy, face-planting drunk. And I didn't want to do it alone.

After Teresa grabbed her skateboard from the back of the coat closet, we headed for the fridge. There was a twelve-pack in there from who knows when. It was, in fact, the only thing in there. With a big grin, Teresa stuffed a few cans into the pockets of her hoodie.

I did the same, but I also pulled out my keys, punctured a hole in the bottom of one of the remaining cans, and shotgunned the thing.

Teresa giggled. "I've never seen you do that."

I shrugged. "First time for everything."

We wandered out into the parking lot. At the bottom of the stairs, Teresa threw her skateboard onto the asphalt and kicked off. When she turned and gave me a little wave, I felt a throb in the very center of my guts. I realized how much I missed those days when she wore the same pair of jeans for days on end and spent the weekend riding her skateboard up and down in front of our building.

For the rest of the afternoon, I watched Teresa zip around the lot. Slumped against the concrete wall with a beer in my hand, I was truly at peace for the first time in weeks. The cheap brew bubbled through my veins and into my brain and gave me that warm, woozy feeling that only beer can. At the same time, the familiar sound of Teresa's wheels dragging against the pavement soothed my nerves.

When Teresa finished riding, I followed her back inside the apartment and we finished off the last couple of cold ones in the fridge. We crushed the cans and threw them at each other. We had fun. Just like we used to. You know—before things got weird.

~ ~ ~

When the sky was just hinting of dusk, Teresa claimed she just wanted to "rest her eyes." But after about three seconds with her head on the arm of the couch, she was out. I laid a blanket over her, then stepped back to watch. She was breathing slow and deep, like babies do, and I thought I'd rather die than wake her. At the same time, I wished she had waited just a little longer to pass out. I didn't want to be alone with my thoughts, and I knew I couldn't take any pills to help me sleep. It would be too dangerous with all the alcohol coursing through my system.

So I just sat on the far end of the couch in my stupid, lonely apartment. Every time I closed my eyes, I saw Charlie coming to the door. Charlie talking to me like I wasn't a rival, but just some kid brother type from Jessa's "small town."

There was Jessa. Idiotic Jessa, who started thinking of me as a child again as soon as she shacked up with that big shot. If she had just let me be instead of sending Charlie with his vague, patronizing offer of "help," I would have forgotten all about her. She would have been a distant memory to me.

I glanced at Teresa, curled up on the couch like a fucking angel. If Charlie hadn't come around with his questions and his accusations, I would have forgotten about Jessa and it would have been just me and Teresa. You know, the two of against the world and all that. But Jessa couldn't mind her business.

And now I couldn't sleep, and Teresa was out cold, and I didn't have anybody to talk to. I didn't want my family to know how shitty my life had become, and I couldn't trust Matt to keep his mouth shut. My only option, I decided, was to give Jessa a piece of my mind. She deserved it, that was for sure. And once I said my piece, I might have a shot at getting some rest. It would be easy. There was no reason to sit there in my living room another minute.

Chapter 29

I was out the door in a second. I unlocked my bike and pulled it out from its place behind the stairs. Then I was on the streets, peddling like mad under the flotilla of clouds that had gathered while I was inside. A spitting rain pelted me like little needles, but I didn't care—I was stupid ugly drunk, and I was wired. I ripped down Franklin until I reached Los Feliz. Large, whimsically appointed homes rose up in front of me. Wild gardens spilled over tall iron fences. Plaster cherubs pissed cheerfully into giant seashells.

When I caught sight of a street sign bearing the name Charlie had marked on the back of his business card I made a sharp left, pedaling hard up the hill. I scanned the curb for house numbers, and there it was—number 2120. I pressed on the brakes, hydroplaned, and skidded to a stop.

As soon as I looked up, I knew why the practical princess had moved in. Charlie's erstwhile rental property was straight out of a fucking fairy story. The place was old and settled and whitewashed, with a slanted set of stone steps leading up to the door. I chuckled as I tossed my bike into the bushes and raced up the stairs. Jessa had probably gone running out of her generic North Hollywood unit the second Charlie showed her a photograph.

I pounded hard on the front door, which was much larger and more solid than it had seemed from the street. There was no answer, but something inside me assured me Jessa was there. It was like I could smell her from the street. Unwilling to be ignored, I picked up an ornamental rock from inside one of the planters and banged it against the door as hard as I could. Paint fell off in big flakes, then in chunks.

Just when I was sure the old door would crack down the middle, I heard the distinctive scrape of a window being opened. When I looked up, there was Jessa, leaning out of the gable window at the top of the house. Her too-green eyes stared into my bloodshot ones with surprise and a little fear. By then, I knew what I was there to do, and I was sure she did too. There was no love in my heart. Just spite. And want of revenge. And an animal desire.

Jessa left her place at the window. Then she appeared at the door. "You shouldn't be here. Not now," she insisted. But her voice was meek. A little mouse voice.

"So tell me to go."

She couldn't. She didn't. She was already reaching out for me. Even though I was skinny and disgusting and probably reeked like the rat-hole I lived in.

Taking big strides, I backed her inside. Jessa stumbled against the stairs, and then I was on her. My hands were everywhere. My tongue was in her mouth. But she never pushed me away. She only opened my mouth wider with hers. Her hands were in my hair.

"What about our friend Charlie?" I asked.

"You know nothing else matters when it's you, Law. Even though you're closer to unlovable than I've ever imagined you could be."

She was pretty as always. She was fucking beautiful. And she couldn't say no to me and she couldn't let go of me. And she was mine.

~ ~ ~

When I got home the next morning, I felt very hollow. All I wanted was to be alone, but then there was Teresa right in the living room. Waiting.

"Where were you all night?" she cried out.

I shook my head. "Doesn't matter."

When I headed for the kitchen, Teresa was on my heels. "Of course it matters, Law. I don't understand. Everything was so good between us yesterday. We were running around and having fun just like we used to, and . . ."

"None of that matters either. We're broken up."

"What? Because of *her*?"

"It's not that. I don't care about her." I opened the refrigerator and rooted around for something to eat. I couldn't remember the last time I had consumed something with nutritional value.

"Then why would you want to be apart?"

"Just let me go, Teresa," I said. I guess I sounded so exhausted—so utterly *done*—that she didn't try to debate me.

"Well, I can't move out!" She quaked. "Not now."

"I'm not moving either."

"So what am I supposed to do? Go on sleeping in your bed? How can you ask for something like that, Lawson?"

"We have a couch."

Teresa let out a strangled scream.

I knew I'd blindsided her. I knew it was cruel. But I also knew that I wasn't finished with Jessa. Not by a long shot. Charlie, in his utter, insulting ignorance, had left her there for the taking. And every time I had her, it would be a direct, personally addressed message about how stupid and selfish she was. As for Charlie . . . well, I was pretty sure it would knock him down a notch or two.

Chapter 30

The next time the mood took me, I called Jessa and demanded she come and pick me up. For some reason, she did. Not ten minutes later, there was Charlie's zippy little Beemer idling at the curb.

When we got to Charlie's house Jessa and I headed up the steps nearly a minute apart. Neither of us was keen on broadcasting our sordid little affair to the neighbors. But the second we got inside, we were like a couple of animals, grinding in the hallway and pinning each other against the wall. It was disgusting, really.

Our horny coupling went on for the rest of the day and into the night. When I was spent, I stretched out on Charlie's California king and got the first real, deep, natural sleep I'd had in a very long time. At home, I could never get a moment's rest. Teresa always wanted to know where I was, how I was. She was always desperate for my attention. Begging me to "just talk to her."

Jessa did nothing of the kind. She never hassled me with questions, or tried to press me into conversation. It was a big relief to be around somebody who honestly didn't give a shit about me. Finally, I could relax.

~ ~ ~

Whenever Jessa and I were inside Charlie's place, we were pieces of meat to each other. The things we did in that house—the way we treated each other—was deplorable. And yet, it seemed to satisfy something deep inside both of us. Jessa and I weren't so different, really. We did what we wanted. We took what we could get. We didn't care who lost out.

Anytime, day or night, Jessa came when called to collect me in Charlie's sick ride. Even as I became more disgusting by the day. I never combed my hair, and I couldn't remember the last time I'd changed my shirt. I wasn't good company either. I barely spoke. I made unreasonable demands: fresh coffee in the wee hours. Specific and sometimes complicated sexual favors.

"What do you get out of this?" I asked Jessa late one night. I was all spread out on Charlie's bed, taking up most of the mattress.

Jessa was curled up in a ball, facing the wall. I wasn't even sure that she was awake. But then she spoke out into the darkness. "I guess I keep hoping that one day you'll forgive me," she said.

"For what?"

"For the way I treated you, back in Gunther."

"You really think that's why I don't want to be with you?"

Jessa turned over. "I don't know, Lawson. Why don't you want to be with me? Whenever you're not working, you're here. And I would never treat you badly again. You know how I feel about you."

It was weird. A few times, I had almost believed that Jessa was still in love with me. She certainly made the claim often enough. Then I remembered that Jessa Warlow would never be able to love anyone. She would never be able to care about another person as much as she cared about getting whatever it was she wanted in that moment. Whether that was her big break, or an orgasm. Falling for someone like Jessa—believing her candied words—was beyond dangerous. It was stupid.

~ ~ ~

I suppose all things, even sordid ones, must come to an end. One night, just before I sailed off to dreamland on Charlie's fifty-gazillion thread count sheets, Jessa informed me that she would no longer be coming to fetch me in Charlie's BMW. Or any vehicle, for that matter. Because I had made it abundantly clear how I *didn't* feel about her. And Charlie was coming back the next afternoon.

I made no comment. But in the morning, I didn't get up. I just laid there on my back on Charlie's four-poster in my jeans.

Jessa was already buzzing around the room, readying everything for the big homecoming. Finally, she yanked at the sheets. "Lawson. Get up. You have to go."

I didn't budge. I stared at the vaulted ceiling, which had become intimately familiar to me. I knew every crack, every scratch in the paint. "You're not even going to tell him, are you?"

She sighed. "I'll probably tell him something happened—with an ex-boyfriend—but that it didn't mean anything. I won't tell him the extent of it. Or that it happened here."

"And you're not going to say it happened with me."

"That would just make everything worse and more horrible than it already is, don't you think?"

I remained prostrate and defiant on the bed while Jessa tidied up the room. Then she grabbed for the sheets a second time. "Law, please. I need to clean these before Charlie gets back!"

I crossed my arms over my chest. "I think I ought to stay. I'll tell Charlie I might not handle a guitar like a man, but I sure handled his girl like one."

Jessa rolled her eyes. She knew I was too chickenshit to wait around for Charlie. While I pouted, she rummaged in her purse and tossed a couple of crisp twenties my way. "Cab fare."

"Drive me," I insisted. But Jessa was already on the phone with a taxi service. Grudgingly, I peeled myself off the bed and slunk outside to wait for a car under a blistering noontime sun.

I hadn't bothered searching for my shirt, so I got a nasty sunburn on my neck and shoulders. The cab's rough seat, repaired in a few places with duct tape, only made it worse.

~ ~ ~

When I finally got home, I was in no mood to have anyone on my case. But then there was Teresa on my heels as usual like some yapping little terrier.

"Where have you been?" she kept asking. As if she didn't know.

When I retreated into the bathroom to splash cool water on the back of my neck, I checked myself out in the mirror—and immediately regretted it. I was pale and ugly. My cheeks were sunken, too, which always made my teeth look really terrible. They just seemed bigger in my face. Longer. Like rat teeth. I wondered how anybody could stand looking at me.

I didn't think Teresa would be so bold as to follow me into the john. But she did.

I scowled into the mirror. In that moment, I hated her more than anybody in the world—more than Jessa Warlow, or Charlie, or even my father. I hated her for caring about me and refusing to give up on me. That was the worst thing you could do to somebody like me.

"Law, you need help," Teresa whined. "I'm worried about you."

I bristled. *As if Teresa had room to talk.* Little druggie-dropout that she was. "Mind your business, meth mouth," I snapped. It was a much-used invective at Pizza Kitchen, and I tossed it without thinking.

Teresa positioned herself to reply, and internal alarms ripped through me like air raid sirens. I knew what she was going to say. Even if Teresa was the one who took drugs sometimes, I was the one with the fucked-up grill. I knew that, but I couldn't hear Teresa say it. Not in that moment. Not with the kind of morning I was having.

In one desperate motion meant to quiet Teresa, and the whole world, I jabbed my fist into the mirror. The cheap glass cracked and shattered and the pieces went tinkling into the sink. My knuckles bled down my arm. And then I was just staring into the mirror, shocked at how much blood I'd managed to produce with a single, unplanned motion. I was struck dumb.

Teresa broke the silence. "I wasn't going to say what you think I was going to say," she told me in a voice so light and gentle and truthful that it shook me to the core. "Why are you so angry, Lawson?"

My mouth fell open, but I could form no words. I had no answer. While I stood there bleeding Teresa calmly fetched a pair of tweezers and some bandages. She gestured for me to sit down on the closed lid of the toilet. I obeyed and, very carefully, she tweezed shards of glass out of my knuckles and wrapped up my hand with gauze.

Finally, I found words. "Thank you," I choked out.

Teresa nodded. And, all at once, something changed in me. Like the flick of a switch. The rage inside me slept. I was no longer on high alert, ready to snap the second something didn't go my way.

From that day on, I could stand to be around Teresa. I could stand to be at home. When I wasn't working, Teresa and I spent our time nestled on the couch, watching movies on her tablet. Even if the movie turned out to be something really shitty, it didn't matter. I just lay back and let the bland storylines run through my head. It kept my mind quiet. I didn't say much, but Teresa wasn't bothered. Because at least I wasn't out all night, nutting in some other woman.

I let Jessa go. She disappeared from my memory. I never thought of her. And Teresa, wisely, never spoke her name. Life went on. And on. As it does. Whether you really want it to or not.

Chapter 31

I never planned to see or speak to Jessa Warlow again. By all appearances, she had the same idea about me. Months passed, and she never called or showed up at my place. She didn't send Charlie over to interrogate me either—thank god. The silence between us was truly beautiful.

That's why I was so disappointed when, one afternoon, her number flashed on my caller ID. That was clearly in violation of our unspoken no-contact pact. Still, I wasn't worried or thrown off by her sudden intrusion. I knew I didn't want Jessa in my life, and I wasn't afraid to let her know it.

"Jessa. Please don't call me," I told her when I picked up the phone.

Jessa paused. "I know you don't want to talk to me, Lawson. But something's come up. Something . . . unexpected." Her voice was strangely businesslike.

"If this is about the record, do whatever you like. Distribute it, sell it, scrap it if that's what you want to do," I told her. "It's immaterial to me."

"Please trust me, Lawson," Jessa said breezily. "This is important. I just need fifteen minutes of your time. In person."

I figured Charlie had come up with a placement for one of her songs. Maybe on a show at his network. He was no dummy. He knew his future with Jessa was riding on his contributions to her supposed career. Most likely, I'd have to sign a few papers releasing my rights to the record. If that was what I had to do to wash my hands of the whole business, I was ready.

"Okay," I agreed. "I'll meet you at noon tomorrow. At the picnic tables by Heavenly Donuts. You'll have fifteen minutes."

After I hung up the phone, Teresa crept into the living room. "Who was that?" she asked.

"Jessa."

She winced.

"Don't worry. I'm just meeting her to sign away my rights to our music. If it's something more than that—if Jessa and Charlie want any further work done on the record—they'll have to take it to another studio. I don't even want my name on it."

"Won't Tim be disappointed?" Teresa ventured. "Even angry?"

"It doesn't matter. I'm finished. With Jessa. And Charlie. And everything that might connect me to Jessa or Charlie. Including that record we made. *Especially* that record we made."

~ ~ ~

The next day, I headed down to the mini mall on the corner. Sure enough, there was Jessa, standing under the bright blue sky in big, dark glasses and some long, beachy dress that I'd never seen her in before. The whole world was so sunny and brilliant that it seemed fake. Like so much plastic stacked pointlessly together.

I couldn't read anything through Jessa's sunglasses, but she wasn't smiling.

"All right," I said, "what exactly do you want me to do?"

She hesitated. "Let's go inside. I'll buy you lunch before we talk. You look like you need it."

"I'm not hungry."

"Okay. Then let's just take a seat right here."

I sat down at the nearest table, and Jessa ducked inside

the donut shop. When she reappeared and handed me a miniature carton of orange juice, I accepted it.

Jessa stared at me, her lips set in a very straight line. At least I thought she was staring at me. It was hard to tell with her big glasses covering half of her face.

"Lawson, I'm going to have a baby," she told me finally. And then she was silent.

That one I didn't expect. I tried not to peer down at her abdomen, which was mostly obscured anyway by her weird hippie dress. "That's great for you," I muttered. "I hope Charlie's happy." I pretended to be very busy with my OJ.

"No, he's not very happy, Lawson."

I picked at the carton. Little orange dots collected underneath my fingernails. "Why the hell not? He's rich, and he's obsessed with you. Why wouldn't he want you to start bearing the heirs to his fortune?"

"Lawson."

"What?"

"The baby's not his."

I had to laugh at that one. "Jesus, really? So you're already fucking around on him again."

"No, not again."

"What do you mean?"

Jessa cocked her chin. "Are you just pretending not to get it?"

But then I did get it. And my head was spinning. I spit out my last gulp of orange juice into the dirt. "How do you know? I mean, how do you know it's mine?"

"The timing, first of all. And . . . well, we weren't careful, Lawson. You know that."

I stared hard at the ground, which was mostly dirt covered with a few patches of yellow grass. Slowly, I began to accept the possibility of what Jessa had said. And then the probability. "Well . . . what do you want from me?" I asked.

"I don't want anything from you. I just thought you should be aware of the situation. So you could decide what to do, or not do. I wanted to be fair to you."

I shook my head. "I don't know what to say. I mean, I can't be a parent, Jessa. Not with you. And not in general. It's just . . . it's not in me. It's not even in my heart."

"That's what I figured."

I still couldn't see Jessa's eyes through her sunglasses. It was making me sort of nuts, but I didn't want to touch her. Finally, I gave in and took the glasses off. When I looked her in the eyes, I saw that it was all true and no joke.

I tossed her sunglasses onto the table. "I have to go."

"No problem," she said.

Her words got me right in the gut. I couldn't stand it. Nothing was ever a problem for her. Terrible things happened and she was just the same Jessa, headstrong and indestructible and never afraid. Nothing could break her. Nothing could even touch her.

Jessa left first. From my spot at the picnic table I watched her amble over to her car. It was new and bland. Definitely a rental. *I guess daddy took the T-bird away*, I thought to myself in an inward attempt at humor. But I couldn't even laugh at my own joke. When my insides heaved, I turned my eyes away and headed home. At the corner, I threw a sloppy left into the stop sign and busted my knuckles open again.

All I could think was that the universe was really sick. Of all the times for an accident like that to happen. Some miracle of life . . . a baby conceived in carelessness. That was no beginning for any kid. I felt really sorry for him. *Babies*, I thought, *should only come to people like Matt's sister Sarah and her husband*. They should be with people who cared about each other. They shouldn't come to people like me and Jessa.

Jessa couldn't break my heart anymore, but that baby broke my heart. I couldn't help shedding a few tears. By the time I reached my building I was full-on blubbering, with my face going hot and snot running down my nose and everything. I didn't have the energy to clean off my knuckles properly, so I just wiped the blood all over my shirt.

When I let myself into the apartment, Teresa gasped. "My god, Lawson. What happened?"

Of course she was the last person on earth I could tell. "Leave. Please!" I half-ordered, half-begged. "I need to be alone."

I guess I seemed just desperate—or crazed—enough that Teresa got out of my way and started gathering her things.

I kept on moving. Into the bedroom and into bed, where I pulled all the covers over my head. When I heard the front door click shut, I knew I was alone at last. But it was no relief. As I laid there under the blankets, breathing the stuffy air and leaking tears and blood, all I could think about was that baby. With the way I turned out, the kid was screwed. I was going to be an absentee father like my dad had been. Besides that, I wasn't even a good guy anymore . . . hadn't been for a long time. I was reckless. I was mean. I didn't care about anybody—not even myself. Not really.

I lay there, dazed, in a gray purgatory for the rest of the day. After dark, the nightmares came, with visions of helicopters and SWAT teams chasing me down, bent on capturing me so I could stand trial for crimes too unspeakable to name. I tossed and turned. I sweated through the blankets.

When the sun was just hinting of morning, I heard Teresa come in. She tiptoed into the room and slipped quietly under the covers next to me.

At first, I was soothed by the familiar weight of her forearm across my sternum. Then I realized what her presence meant. Questions I didn't want to answer. Answers that would hurt her, maybe more than I'd hurt any other person.

The coming day loomed ahead of me like some great beast lying in wait. A beast I could not avoid—unless I acted quickly. I racked my brain. I needed a plan. And then, very suddenly, I had one. It had been right there in front of me all the time. The energy of my inspiration gave me the strength to raise my limbs. The fog in my mind lifted. For the first time in months, I practically shot out of bed, ready to take on the day.

Clumsy with my eagerness, I lurched toward the living room. I grabbed my hoodie, and Teresa's keys, and stumbled up the stairs to the studio. Knowing Tim and Lydia might be asleep behind their bedroom door, I unlocked the door and entered very quietly and crept over to Tim's desk.

With a birthday-party level of excitement, I jiggled the bottom drawer and slid it open. In the very back of the drawer, just where he said I'd find it, was Tim's pistol.

I picked it up and turned it over in my hands with a feeling of wonder. The cold metal was sickly green in the pre-dawn light and, truth be known, I didn't like touching it. But that, I figured, was some tough luck. So I picked up the hunk of metal, stuck it in my pocket, and went gliding down the stairs.

Teresa's car was waiting for me in the parking lot like an old friend. Everything was working out so well, and going so smoothly, that I was sure I was simply living out some ancient destiny. When Teresa suddenly ran out into the back lot, skidding to a stop at the top of the stairs, I wasn't fazed.

"Law, where are you going?"

I looked up. Teresa was prettier than I'd ever seen her. Her tea-colored eyes were bright and clear. The light—gray and yellow at the same time—painted her elfin features a sallow gold.

"Santa Monica," I told her. I didn't have to lie. Seeing as I was effectively stealing Teresa's car, she couldn't follow me. If she tried to take the bus, she'd never get there fast enough. Not in a million years. I felt light and happy. I felt free.

Teresa frowned. "What are you going to do?"

"I'm going to play on the fucking monkey bars, Teresa." I grinned. For once, I didn't care who saw every stupid tooth in my jack-o'-lantern mouth.

Her shoulders sunk. "Lawson, you don't have to choose. I'm serious. If you need to be with her sometimes—I don't mind. I can take it. Whatever you need . . ."

"I don't need her," I interrupted. "I don't need anybody."

"Come inside and we'll call her. You can lie down and I'll make you coffee—extra strong, like you like it—and, when she gets to the apartment, I'll let you be," Teresa promised. "I swear."

But I was already getting in the car. It was too late for Teresa's pleas. Or anybody's, for that matter. With a final salute, I fired up Teresa's Crown Victoria and maneuvered onto the road.

Chapter 32

At Cahuenga, I pulled onto the wide open freeway. There was no traffic so early on a Saturday morning. It was just me and the first rays of golden California sun glittering under the gray of the marine layer.

As soon as I passed the 405, I could smell the ocean. When I cracked the windows, salty air rushed through my sinuses and gave me a clarity I could never get in the lung-clogging smog of Hollywood. Seconds later, I saw signs for Santa Monica. As I exited, all my limbs were tingling with what I guess was anticipation.

At the pier, I turned left and headed south until the street dead-ended behind the boardwalk. I nosed up to the very end of the asphalt and turned off the engine. Practically glowing with energy, I grabbed some crumpled notebook paper and a pen from the glove box, shoved them in my pocket, and headed for the seaside.

I savored the moment my shoes stopped striking concrete and instead sank into the soft, fine sand. All the way down to the shore I dragged my feet so the grains would pour in and out of my Adidas Gazelles.

~ ~ ~

They say the West Coast has shitty sunrises, but the dawning sky was huge in front of me and putting on more of a show than I could have anticipated. Streaks of fuchsia burned through the billowing gray clouds while crackling embers smoked on the horizon. It made me feel awed and quiet.

The beach was exquisite in its solitude. It was just me, the big showoff sky, and the gray suede sea. As I sat cross-legged in the sand with my hood pulled up against the cool bite of morning I set about penning a note to Allison. All I needed to tell her was that she was going to be great. That she didn't need me anymore. And that, unfortunately, I hadn't turned out the way I'd hoped. Of course I wouldn't have to explain to Allison that, sometimes, having a part-time father is worse than having no dad at all. She would already know.

When I finished, I signed my name, stuck the note in my shoe for safekeeping, and got down to business. I figured out how to release the safety pretty quick. I mean, I don't know much about guns, but I'm not an idiot or anything. Then I turned the pistol around, stuck it in my mouth, and squeezed my eyes shut.

Ready to go, so to speak, I pulled the trigger without fanfare. If anything, I was in a rush.

~ ~ ~

When I died, I didn't hear anything. The world just went black. It was like sleeping with my eyes closed. And then it was like dreaming with my eyes open. When I lifted my gaze, I saw some version of Jessa, kneeling and peering at me very sadly. Her hair streamed behind her in the wind.

I sat up slowly and it/she extended a hand. "Are you going to take me to heaven?" I asked. It was a weird question because I had never really believed in a heaven. I guess the angelic version of Jessa in front of me was pretty convincing.

When she extended her hand, I took it and let our fingers wrap together. And then she reached for the other one. But when I lifted it, it felt strangely encumbered. That's when I realized I was still clutching Tim's pistol. I released my grip and Jessa took the gun out of my hand. She placed it gingerly down onto the sand and pressed my knuckles, all scabby and split, against her cheek. Her eyes were shut against the wind.

It was a long time before either of us said anything. "How are you here?" I choked.

"Teresa called me. She knew I could reach you faster than she could. Also, she thought that maybe you would talk to me."

"And I didn't die?" By then, I was pretty sure. But I wanted to hear it from Jessa.

"No, Lawson. The gun isn't loaded," she explained gently. "I spoke to Tim right after Teresa called me. He said he'd never leave a loaded weapon just lying there in a drawer. You must have passed out."

"Oh. Shit." It made sense, I guess. I hadn't had anything but coffee since that OJ Jessa bought me outside the donut shop.

I wasn't sure what to say, or what to think. But then there wasn't time to do either. Because, all of a sudden, Jessa was looking over my head. She squinted at me guiltily.

"Lawson. I'm sorry. I had to call."

When I turned around, I saw two uniformed officers ambling down the beach.

Chapter 33

I was sure the cops would lock me up, but they didn't. At least, not in jail. Instead, they cuffed me and drove me to a psych facility for one of those seventy-two hour observations—a 5150.

I'm sure being committed to a mental health facility can be a harrowing experience, but for me it was a loping stroll toward the boardwalk, a nonchalant officer saying "In the back, bud," and then a long drive up the 405.

That drive ended at a campus north of the city with a large, disinfectant-smelling lobby. There, a woman behind a clear plastic barrier copied down some information from my driver's license and a man who looked like somebody's grandfather asked me several canned questions—mostly concerning whether I had any further intentions to hurt myself or others. I gave all the right answers. Not because I meant them—I wasn't sure of that yet—but because I didn't want to give anybody an excuse not to let me out.

After a young clinician checked my head for lice and took my shoelaces and hoodie away, he showed me to a small room with three plain, neatly made beds. "We're full," he told me. "But I've already asked somebody to bring up a cot."

It was strange. The place seemed exactly like a college dorm. The only difference was, I couldn't leave.

~ ~ ~

By afternoon, I had already scratched the college dorm comparison. The mental ward where I'd ended up was a lot more like grade school. All of the corridors led to a wide open "main room" done up in bright colors and stuffed with books and puzzles. There was even a cafeteria, complete with plastic trays.

I never entertained the thought that somebody would try to see me while I was in the hospital. But then, when I was forcing down a bologna sandwich in said cafeteria, the same clinician who showed me to my room informed me I had a visitor.

I could feel the panic beginning to rise in my guts, right alongside all that bologna. The survival strategy I'd settled on mainly depended on keeping my brain empty and then, at some indeterminate point in the future, figuring out how to face the world, and my life. Visitors didn't factor into that plan.

I hoped like hell that my as-yet-unnamed caller was not Teresa. Teresa, the person I'd hurt the most. The person most deserving of a sincere and well thought out apology. The person I was least prepared to see.

To my immense relief, it was Jessa who showed up in my room not ten minutes later. Once, I had hated her so hard for her refusal to be rattled. I'd been maddened and frustrated by her eternal cool. This time, those were the most appealing things about her. I wouldn't have to worry about saying something that might offend her or send her into a torrent of tears. I could breathe easy.

"Hey there," Jessa said, "the gentleman in scrubs said we could stay in here. As long as we keep the door open." In her casual way, Jessa hopped up next to me on my cot. Like it was any other day. Like we were anywhere else.

It was weird seeing her wearing the same dress and jacket she was wearing back on the beach. The morning already felt like a million years ago.

"Is it all right that I'm here?" she asked.

"Sure. I'm just surprised anybody wants to see me. After what I did, and the way I've been acting."

"Lawson, all your friends care about you. No matter what. I'm not the only one who was here. Tim drove up as soon as I told him where you were. He stuck around for a few hours, but the powers that be wouldn't let anybody in until a few minutes ago."

I sucked in air through my teeth. I'd broken Tim's trust. He was the last person I expected to make an appearance at my bedside. "He didn't have to do that."

"He wanted to. Tim knows you only stole from him because you were desperate. That you weren't yourself. He even said you can stay with him when you get out. For as long as you need."

I could tell Jessa thought I would welcome this news, but I knew that if Tim was offering me a place to crash, it meant Teresa didn't want me coming home. I shouldn't have been so shocked. After all that had happened, and everything I'd done. But, somehow, I was.

Jessa saw my face fall. "Wait . . ." She backpedaled. "I didn't mean . . ."

"I get it," I interrupted. "It's okay." It wasn't really *okay*, of course, but I wanted Jessa to know I wasn't going to lose it again. I didn't know much, but I did know that I was going to keep it together—no matter what.

Jessa nodded, then looked me over as if deciding whether she should say more.

"What is it?" I asked.

"Well, I think you should know that I called Allison and told her you're in here." Her eyes crinkled guiltily, the way they had when the cops had started their tromp across the sand.

"Thank you," I said softly. I hadn't spoken with Alli for weeks. Maybe more than that. Losing touch with Alli may not have been my worst offense, but it was one I could set right. One I would set right. As soon as I got permission to use one of the telephones I'd seen lined up evenly in a hallway near the cafeteria.

~ ~ ~

Just when I was starting to wonder at the lack of psychoanalyzing on the psych ward, I was called to a room on the first floor. A middle-aged psychiatrist with bobbed gray hair and alert eyes met me at the door.

She asked a lot more questions than the grandpa at admissions. She wanted to know about what happened on the beach, and why. Something about her was disarming. Maybe it was the toes of her Birkenstocks peeking out from the bottom of her scrubs. I told her everything. About Jessa, and the baby, and my family back at home.

When I was finished, she peered at me through her tortoise shell eyeglasses.

"I know what you're going to say," I told her defensively. "That I'm crazy. Like my mother."

"What I think," she said, "is that you're too hard on yourself. Sounds like you've always been the hero. The good guy. The bearer of burdens. Well, nobody's perfect. My advice to you is to be honest with yourself about what you want, and then be honest with the people around you."

"That's it?"

"That's it for now. I can prescribe you something to help you relax, but I don't plan to start you on anti-depressants. It will take two weeks to see any effects, and it's best if you have an outpatient psychiatrist who can manage your dosage. Anyway . . ." The doctor was already getting up, pushing her chair back into the corner of the room. "That's all the time we have today," she said. "Sorry. This is county."

~ ~ ~

As soon as I figured out how to use the phones, which featured a complicated dial-out system, I called Allison. The phone rang over and over, with the same shrill bleat. I was just about to give up when, suddenly, Allison picked up.

"Alli," I said before she could even get out a *hello*. "It's me."

"Oh my god. Lawson," she breathed. "I can hardly believe it."

I wasn't sure where to begin. I wasn't sure how much she knew. I wasn't sure how much she wanted to know. "How are you?" I asked finally.

"I'm fine, Lawson. How are you?"

"I'm okay too. I'm sorry that I stopped answering the phone. Or calling you back."

"I'm sorry that I didn't know anything was wrong. I really thought you were just busy," she whispered. "Can you tell me what happened?"

I only realized my hands were trembling when the telephone went tumbling right out of them. It swung like a pendulum on its thick metal cord until I picked it up again. "Still there?"

"Right here."

"All right. The thing is . . . Jessa's going to have a baby."

"Oh." Alli paused. "I didn't even know she was seeing anybody."

"She's not. At least, right now she's not." I cleared my throat. The next part was harder to say, but I wasn't going to chicken out. I remembered what the doctor said about being honest. "It's mine, Alli. We—me and Jessa—didn't mean for it to happen. But it did."

I closed my eyes while I waited for her reaction. I was prepared for disappointment. Admonishments. Gasps of incredulity and judgment. Instead, Allison shrieked into the phone.

"Oh my god. I'm so happy! I can't believe you're having a little baby. My brother is having a baby. I'm going to be an aunt!"

Allison's joy was an utter surprise and a revelation to me. I couldn't believe how differently two people could see the same situation. When I heard about that baby, I thought it was the worst thing that ever happened. Allison just felt . . . delight.

~ ~ ~

That evening, I asked for special permission to make a second phone call. It couldn't wait any longer. I had to speak to Teresa. I couldn't take back the things I'd done, no matter how much I wanted to. But it wasn't my right to simply disappear. The way I saw it, Teresa was the one who should decide how things should end. If she wanted me to get lost, I would. If she wanted to scream in my face or question me for hours so she could get some kind of closure, I would endure the tirade or the interrogation.

And yet neither tirade or interrogation was to be. Because, after I dialed, somebody else's voice hissed into my ear. "Yessssss?"

"Dylan."

"Lawson," he said, with surprise and no little disgust. "Didn't think you'd have the nerve to call."

"Well, I did. And I'm glad you're over at the apartment." I really was. I'd written Dylan off as a troublemaker, but he always had Teresa's best interests at heart. He was looking out for her all along. He was right to be suspicious of me.

"Teresa didn't want to be alone after what happened," he explained.

"Right. Well, is she there? I'd like to talk to her."

"She's not in at the moment. She's at her parents' place."

"Oh. I didn't think she was speaking to her parents."

"After everything that's gone on, the kind of things that used to seem important—like her parents hating the way she dressed in high school—aren't quite so significant. You get me?"

"Yeah, I get you." I knew just how wrong I'd done Teresa. I had cheated on her, of course, but I'd also done much worse. I clung to her past the point when things were already over. At first because I really believed we could make it work. But then I'd only used her as a kind of human shield against Jessa Warlow, who I didn't want to love. Who I couldn't admit that I loved.

Dylan paused. "You know what? I should tell you the rest. Teresa's friends, and her family, all think it's best if she doesn't talk to you anymore. I don't have to tell you why, do I? Everyone's encouraging her to forget about you."

"Okay." I swallowed. "I won't try to contact Teresa. But if things change, she's welcome to call me anytime. Tim knows how to reach me."

"Why'd you do it anyway?" Dylan asked.

I knew what he meant, and I decided to answer truthfully. It was up to Dylan what he wanted to relay to Teresa. He'd know better than me what she could handle, and when. "I found out I had a kid on the way."

Dylan snorted. "Jesus. You really are a fuck-up, Lawson."

"Maybe," I said. "But I'm not going to fuck this up." As soon as I said the words, I knew I meant them. I wanted to be a part of that baby's life. I didn't want to bail on him. My dad had done a shit job, but that didn't mean I couldn't do better.

I decided then and there. I *would* do better. Even if I didn't have all the answers, I would figure it out. And Jessa would be there to help.

Chapter 34

On my final evening as a prisoner of the ward, Jessa showed up again. This time she didn't sit down. "So," she said from the doorway of my room, "you're out of here tomorrow."

"Guess I haven't done anything to piss off the jailers. The guy who guards the urinals even slipped me a few nicotine patches for good behavior. Apparently, they're like currency around here."

Jessa managed an obligatory laugh, but I could tell she didn't feel like joking. She parted her lips as if to speak, then shook her head.

"What is it?" I asked.

She sighed. "I want to know if you'll come stay with me, Lawson. Just until you get back on your feet. Tim made that kind offer to stay at his place, of course, but we both know he doesn't have the space."

"It's kind of you to offer, too, Jessa. But I can't live with Charlie." I shrugged. "I'll stay at a motel until I find a new apartment. You don't have to worry about me."

"Oh." Jessa cocked her chin. "Didn't I tell you? I'm not at Charlie's place anymore."

"Really?"

"I'm renting a bungalow on my own. Because . . ." Jessa hesitated. "Well, because of the baby."

I stared at my shoes. "I guess Charlie wasn't too pleased when he found out."

"He wasn't angry exactly. More like very, very surprised. I guess, in his mind, you were the last . . ." Jessa stopped herself. "Anyway, Charlie didn't throw me out. He slept on the couch the night I told him and then, in the morning, he marched into the kitchen declaring that he wants to work things out. That he would raise the baby with me. You know, like it was his next project."

For the first time since she arrived, I looked Jessa straight in the eye. "You told him no, right?"

She turned and stared out of the window at the far end of the room. "Of course."

~ ~ ~

In the morning, I met with my Birkenstocks-wearing doctor for the second and final time. After a twenty minute interview, she approved my release, and I was a free man. My belongings were returned to me in a brown paper bag and I was sent back into the world. Even though I'd only been confined three days, it still felt strange to stroll right out of the hospital doors when I'd required supervision to take a leak just the day before. I hoped I was ready, but it wasn't like I had a choice. I'd never signed up for medical insurance, and I was sure there was already a fat bill in the mail for the three days I spent on lockdown.

Paper bag in hand, I stood on the curb in the hazy morning sunshine waiting for Jessa to appear. And then there she was in her shiny, colorless rental car.

"Where we headed?" I asked as I climbed in.

Jessa pulled out onto the road and headed for the freeway. "Tujunga."

I was glad to hear it. At that particular moment in my life, I wanted to be far from the frantic pace and the chaos of L.A. I wanted to be somewhere quiet. At least until I got my head straight.

"You still talk to Charlie?" I asked as a few motorcycles buzzed by, racing toward the mountains.

Jessa kept her eyes on the road. "Sometimes. What makes you ask that?"

I was on a mission, to set as many things right as I could. "I want to refund him for the record," I told Jessa. "As soon as possible." I didn't like the idea that all Charlie's investment had bought him was a lot of bullshit and betrayal.

Jessa laughed. "Oh, I wouldn't worry about Charlie. He's already on track to make back his investment."

"What do you mean?"

"He got a placement for two of our songs. In a CX network show." She glanced in my direction. "Law, Charlie was disappointed that it didn't work out between me and him, but he's a businessman. He wouldn't stuff an opportunity just because things didn't go the way he thought they would."

I didn't know what to say. It had been so long since I'd had any really good news, I wasn't sure how to react. So I just smiled out the window as Jessa exited the highway and drove through the foothills of Tujunga.

Not thirty seconds later, she pulled up in front of a little house perched twenty feet above the street. It was one of those beige stucco numbers with a Spanish-style roof. Cacti and brightly colored blooms mixed riotously in the garden. Behind it, the dusty mountains rose up against a cloudless sky.

I didn't know how long that house would be my home. Whether I'd be there a few days, a few weeks, or even much longer. There would be time, I knew, to figure all of that out. But, before we went into that house, there was one more thing I wanted Jessa to know.

"Everything I said when I met you on the corner—I didn't mean it," I blurted out. "The baby . . . I want to be there for him."

If Jessa was surprised, she didn't show it. "Her," she corrected as she killed the engine. Then she opened up the door, stepped out of the car, and began moving up the wooden stairs stacked right into the hillside.

When I got out, I had to hold the door to steady myself. I could hardly catch my breath. I understood, of course, that I was going to have a kid. But knowing I would have a daughter made it all that much more real. I was going to be a dad. I didn't know what exactly that would mean for me. Or even how I'd pull it off.

Through the sunlight reflecting off of the stairs, I could just barely make out Jessa's form. Up on the front stoop, she turned around and shaded her eyes.

"You coming up or what?" she called.

For a few seconds, I hesitated. Walking into that house would be like walking into a new era. That was heavy stuff. I looked back up at Jessa, for some kind of sign. Some kind of reassurance that I was doing the right thing.

Jessa grinned down at me. "I mean, you're welcome to sleep outside tonight. Though you might end up dinner for a few coyotes."

The tension was broken. All I could do was shake my head and laugh. And take those steps three at a time.

CPSIA information can be obtained
at www.ICGtesting.com
Printed in the USA
LVHW040859031218
599060LV00002B/83

9 781682 916971